Tiny Acorns

An Anthology
of
New Writing

Edited by Tim Atkinson

Published in 2010 by Dotterel Press
ISBN: 978-0-9562869-1-8

INTRODUCTION

The title of this anthology has, of course, a double meaning. On the one hand, each of the pieces reproduced here might, in time, come to be seen as the moment when a new and mighty oak of writing talent germinated. But the very inspiration for many of these pieces was in itself a tiny, almost insignificant remark made by a disappointed would-be author. Having signed up for a writing class, this student-writer found to her dismay that the course had been cancelled at the last moment due to lack of interest. An equally insignificant (at the time) reply from me suggested – somewhat less than seriously – that I could provide her with an online writing course instead. The momentum grew inexorably, and the result was the introductory writing e-course published first on my blog and now reproduced in the Appendix of this volume. Undeterred by my lack of formal qualifications and relying on the instincts gained through over twenty years of teaching, I crafted a ten week beginner's writing course and watched – fascinated, amazed and pleased – as more and more people signed up.

The fact that so many people signed up so readily for a course run by an unknown quantity, the fact that almost all kept going through the entire ten week run, many submitting exercises and other work to informal 'peer assessment' groups on-line, and the fact that people continued to approach me long after the course has ended proved nothing if not that – for many people – creative writing is a vitally important part of their lives, a means of expression and confession, an activity different from many other hobbies and interests, and something people are prepared to work hard at and improve.

The quality of submissions has been impressive; the result is a varied and entertaining book (the proceeds of which are to be donated to the BBC Children in Need Appeal) covering the genres of fiction, poetry and life-writing and one which I'm sure will appeal to a broad cross-section of readers. And finally, for any budding writers out there, the Appendix contains the full creative writing e-course, inspiration for so many of the pieces published for the first time on the following pages.

Tim Atkinson, November 2010

Contents

The Accident, by Nickie O'Hara

I hung up my work overall, closed the locker door, clicked the padlock shut and walked through the empty, dimly lit shop with the manager, mentally visualising the brown wage packet that was in my handbag. The Saturday job didn't pay much but at least I could afford a trip to the cinema with friends that evening. Once outside, I bid the manager goodbye and, as I strode off across the square, I glanced over my shoulder to see him pocket the bunch of keys and turn towards the car park.

At the bus stop I checked the timetable and saw that I had about seven minutes before the next bus to my village. I pulled my mobile phone from my handbag but remembered that I hadn't topped up the credit yet. I ran across the road and entered the phone box. I dialled a number from memory and spoke to my friend, arranging to meet her in an hour's time.

I replaced the receiver on the hook in the phone box, pushed the door open and then... nothing.

A strange noise; it sounded like a siren.
Voices I didn't recognise, words I didn't understand, a stinging sensation at the top of my head, a pain in my leg - a pain like I'd never felt before, lying down on a hard surface, the flash of lights overhead as I was wheeled down a corridor, plastic curtains, the sound of choking and a voice shouting urgently.

I panicked and tried to sit up but couldn't. Every time I attempted to open my eyes I felt a blinding pain across the top of my head. I could hear someone calling for help in the distance and the urgent movements of people bustling around. Fragmented conversations wafted towards me and then I heard more retching and the sound of liquid being poured into a bucket. I called out but it was only a whisper.

I felt a presence next to me and tried to turn to see who or what it was. That blinding pain shot across the front of my head again. I heard soothing words from a softly spoken person with an Irish lilt,

'It's OK; don't be frightened, you're in hospital. You've been knocked over by a car. Your parents are on their way. I'm just going to have your head and leg X-rayed here. Try not to panic.'

I attempted to open my mouth to speak but she patted my hand and hushed me, telling me to try and relax. I was confused.

A portable X-ray machine was set up next to me and all the time the nurse carried on talking to me, telling me what she was doing. Her comforting voice mollified me and I drifted in and out of sleep. An unusual whirring sound woke me from my slumber and I opened my eyes. Above me was what looked like a rectangular screen with a white cross. I saw a face and cried out in fright. It was distorted, swollen, scraped, bleeding, lop-sided and it had an enormous lump on the forehead. I raised my hand to touch the screen and heard someone shout, 'NO! STAY STILL PLEASE!' I lowered my hand and looked at the screen, trying to work out why I was being shown this image.

I shifted my head slightly to the left. The image in front of me did the same. I blinked and looked again. I twisted my head to the right. The image copied, mimicking my movements. I then realised I was looking at a reflection of myself in the plate of the X-ray machine and I burst into tears. How could that be me? Had I really been knocked over? How had this happened? The salt from my tears ran into the cuts on my face and made me cry out more.

And then I heard a familiar sound.

Echoing down the corridor was the sound of an asthmatic cough that could only belong to my mum. She was here! Finally, something that was recognisable and someone who could make it better. I heard more talking in hushed tones and the swish of plastic curtains. I heard the stifled, throaty gulp of someone attempting to stop themselves from weeping. The X-ray machine was removed from above me and my mum's face came into view. I stared into her eyes, willing her to scoop me up and kiss everything better. She gently held my hand and stroked the uninjured side of my face.

Into the Bliss, by Kirrily Whatman

I had been one of those head down, hopes up parents in the NICU (newborn intensive care unit). I had told myself that nothing would happen to my baby. I was certain of her safety, because she had been the only one of our babies so far who had survived the journey in my womb. She was born and I could see her! My maternal instinct kicked in and I felt I was surely in control of her wellbeing, now that she was here. Yet, despite my stubborn refusal to accept any other outcome, Ellanor slipped through my fingers anyway.

As the weeks passed I waited for some relief from the searing pain inside me. But it never came. My massage therapist compared the impact this was having on my body as being consistent with a car accident victim. I was all at once intrigued and startled by this, as I had not received any physical injury. Still, it seemed my buried grief had manifested itself as a crippling numbness, masking the root cause of the pain below the surface and making it almost impossible for the masseur to provide me with any sense of release.

A year passed, heavy and unbearable in so many ways. Spurring me on was my determination to continually seek meaning and new understanding about Ella's passing, in a way that was both progressive and enriching. Then one morning, I awoke from a sleep that so enlightened me that I struggled to articulate it in my journal. I noted that my memory of my 'sense' of Ellanor was suddenly as strong as it had been all that time ago, long before she had been born or even conceived. We had become so familiar with each other back then, but it had been such a long while since I had tuned in to her light joy and loveliness. It had been shrouded, of course, by my agony over her death, but I realised now that at the heart of what mattered there had always remained – Ellanor.

I was delighted I could still connect with the feelings I had experienced, both for her and from her, in the months prior to her birth. But now, as I brought my awareness into focus in the present, I forced myself to really pay attention to what these feelings were all about. I had to join these two worlds together in my rational mind; wherever it was that Ellanor had gone back to and whatever glimpses she had gifted me needed to merge somehow with my current state of pained existence. But what was this feeling she was giving me?

Then it dawned on me. Bliss. Pure love and bliss. That was all it was. It seemed so simple, yet I also knew that the feeling had been eluding me as I struggled to re-emerge amongst the world. As I sat there on my bed, it became clear to me that I had still been floating during these past months, coming back down from both the high of giving birth and the crushing blow of comprehending that our girl had truly gone, far too soon for my soul to readily accept.

In this emotionally raw state, it was really difficult for me to function and be 'on my game'. Simply being alive had become frightening – I was detached from life but at the same time felt immortal. It was a strange and unnerving place in which I found myself. My husband, Steve, experienced it too; the knowledge that death was no longer the most frightening part about our mortality. Living, surviving our only child – that was our most horrifying fear. And now, we were even living through that, so there seemed nowhere lower to go. Simple tasks, such as making a shopping list, brushing my teeth or hair, having a drink, driving, turning on a radio… every single little mundane thing, the same actions many people would take for granted as they carried them out during the course of their day, became an exhausting, seemingly futile and self-absorbed chore. Debilitating, because they reminded me that I was living my life. I didn't want to do any of these things. They seemed so incredibly indulgent, irrelevant and useless. Each bite of food I ate and, at times, even the breaths I took in and out, weighed very heavily on my guilty, bereft heart — until that day, upon waking and putting my feet on the carpet, a sensation of uplifting lightness came coursing through me, an expression of what must have been some awesome, healing gift during my sleep. Was it really so scary, to confront my mere existence? Was there a way to overcome the overwhelming guilt that I was somehow dishonouring Ellanor by simply being alive when she was not? I began to look at things from a fresh perspective.

Focusing my attention now, I allowed myself to really feel the sensation of the carpet fibres on the soles of my feet. This simple exercise seemed to stir a feeling in me that confirmed — and affirmed — how alive I was. As if I was, for the first time, actually reaching the fibres of my soul. It was undeniable, as easy as allowing me to notice my feet on solid ground and acknowledging what that ground felt like in one, singular moment.I suddenly got it in that instant. The bliss. I had to emerge into the bliss of living.

After that day, I discovered I was able to tune out the distractions that prevented me from knowing my true centre, my own unique bliss, as long as I remembered to seek out the joy in whatever was around me at that moment. The television, banal conversations, even the endless mind chatter I could so easily succumb to, all diverted my attention and it took a great deal of practice to let them wash over me. Instead, I slowly trained myself to notice the beauty and see the natural state of whatever my eyes rested on. Dozens of easily overlooked moments on any given day, like gazing at the clouds drifting overhead as I sat waiting at the traffic lights. Seeing majestic gum trees swaying in the wind. Observing a tiny sparrow as it landed in our garden while I stared out of the window, its only thought being to find its next morsel of nourishment. Watching the dog's paws twitching in her sleep, as if she were dreaming of running. Looking with wonder at the face of the person standing before me and realising the incredible amount of cell divisions, growth, replenishment and adaptation that had taken place during their life so far. I looked at bark on tree trunks and the course of busy ant trails and falling leaves with newfound wonder. None of these beautiful objects of nature had caused my daughter to die. How could I be so heartsore and hurt by the laws of Mother Nature and Father Time, if they could also create such majesty in all living things?

Each aspect of life that I looked at now represented to me a universe within itself. I saw things far more clearly than ever before. For a time, I was even able to look in the faces of adult strangers passing by me in the traffic or at the shops and see what they had looked like as young children. I guess I was glimpsing the child in every single person I came across. I saw their innocence peeking through their facades, a truer version of themselves, perhaps, and it confronted and comforted me all at once.

All of this was utterly breathtaking and comforting to me. Each scene I came across began to reassure me that all would be okay, because all of these merging universes would continue, regardless of whether I fell under, or joined back in and went about my life like I used to before knowing Ellanor, or indeed, now consciously determined to keep my awareness raised in this way.

This time of deep grief, too, would come to pass. I had to bravely trust in that. Besides, there was no other option but to trust. And I was also aware that I had a choice now to see the learning in Ella's death and embrace it, to its fullest conclusion, whatever that would prove to be for me. More than ever, I kept Ellanor's gift steadfast in my sights. It saw me through the hardest times of accepting her passing.

My newfound method of 'back to basics' emptying out became the repeating point of absolute, cleansing zero again for me, in order to fill myself back up again with only those things that gave vitality, not sapped it from me. Here, I could always remind myself that life would continue, no matter whether I liked (or enjoyed) it or not.

Taking my own life was not an option, I realised that now as my feet hit the carpet. But actually living my life? Well, that was not only entirely within my control, it was also my duty to my patient, waiting soul.

Escape, by Nickie O'Hara

Evasive, subtle movements mean that I can
Sidestep the paranoia which faces me and, when I
Circumvent the emotions that manifest whilst
Avoiding that situation, it seems that I can
Pass off my insecurity as
Elusiveness... as always.

The Italian Job, by Sandy Calico

'Nan, can I borrow £469?'

'I'm sorry, Daniel, you know I haven't got that sort of money. If I did I'd buy a new telly. No, love, even if you could pay me back. What's it for anyway?'

'Oh, it doesn't matter. I'll think of something else.'

***

'Nan, can I borrow your extension on Saturday night?'
'Borrow...what?'

'Yes, Nan, your extension, just for the night?'

'Of course you can Daniel. Now, what's this in aid of?'

'Well, you remember I wanted to borrow some money? Well, I wanted to take Sam to Venice for the weekend, but anyway, no one could lend me the money. So I thought I'd bring Venice to Preston.'

'Oh. I see. Right-oh Daniel, it's a grand idea, but how exactly are you going to do that?'

'Well, Nan, I'll be needing your help of course...'

'Don't you always, love.'

'Yes, well, I'm going to cook an Italian meal, well, I may need a bit of help with that, and I want to decorate the extension, you know with flags and that.'

'Oh Daniel, it sounds lovely, how exciting! Young love! I've got a green table cloth. And red serviettes. Oh how exciting! Right, now, let me see. You'll need one of those yokes, y'know a candle in a wine bottle. Jean next door has one. I'm sure she'll lend it to me. Now, you'll need some onions and garlic all strung up...'

'Nan, it's Venice remember, not France.'

'Sorry, I was getting carried away. What's Italian? Pizza, of course, you like those pizza thingies, don't you? I'm sure they've got an offer on at Netto. Buy one get one free, BOGOF. Haha, BOGOF makes me laugh every time. They've got Dr O-something pizzas on offer. We can get two of those...'

'Can we have pasta too, Nan? They have pasta in Italy too.'

'Ooh, Daniel, we'll have to have a look. I'll go tomorrow. I'll get a jar of Dolmio and some spaghetti. It'll be like Lady and the Tramp with you and Sam eating spaghetti! Oh, here I am getting ahead of myself. Who is this Sam, will I meet her on Saturday? Oh no, I suppose you'll want me and your Gramps out of the way. Well, it's Bingo on Saturday night so we'll be out until 10 or so. Anyway, this Sam…'

'You haven't met Sam, Nan.'

'Well that's something to look forward to. So you've got pizza and pasta. Jesus, Mary and Joseph, you'll go bang eating all that!'

'Nan, we've got to have pudding. Ice cream or something'

'Right. So. I'll do my shopping list then: Pizzas (BOGOF), Dolmio, spaghetti, Cornettos…'

'Do they sell Cornettos in Netto, Nan?'

'If they don't, and I'd be surprised if they didn't, I'll treat you to a Viennetta.'

'Thanks Nan, you're the best.'

***

'Daniel love, it's Nan.'

'Hello Nan.'

'So darlin', how did it go? You and Sam hardly touched your pizza and that Dolmio spaghetti wasn't touched at all. You know me and your Gramps won't touch that foreign food. What a waste when there's people starving in Africa. And you disappeared and left me with the washing up too. What on earth was the matter? Did you fall out with Sam?'
'Kind of.'

'What happened love?'

'He turned me down Nan… Nan, say something…Nan!'

'OK. ..so...Ah Daniel... I don't know what to say... He? Oh Lord have mercy... You're still my boy, Daniel. Come round after school tomorrow and we'll eat those Cornettos.'

'Thanks Nan.'

The Trolley, by Steven Herrick-Blake

We found you in tussock, wheels up
like a shot donkey.

Spiders had grown the metal ribs
of your belly shut. Chrome

gleamed beneath the matted poultice
of gnats and bindweed.

Beautiful.

Brushed off we knew the hill and you
were made for one moment.

Down as birds, eye-cornering, swing
across a fast sky.

Quickly you were not made for two.
I barely made it

past the brink

and met the fierce angles of this world
headlong in tall grasses.

My mate tobogganed on and drove
your jolting governance

hard against the sod, laughs flailing
into a cross wind,

inseparable,

your weights ox-ploughing twin grass- tracks
fast through muck and turf -

a railroad of whoops and curses
billowing clock seed

and thistle leaf - until the rough
jerk of wheel pivot

met hidden stone.

In my mind now he doesn't stop
but rattles on, flag

in a long wind getting smaller,
his shouts like copper

on the tongue or an empty basket
dropped

over an edge of years.

As Long As He Needs Me, by Nickie O'Hara

I felt his finger trace my spine from top to bottom. If I'd have been able, I would have let out a sigh of pleasure. I know he only loved me for my inner knowledge and the stories I could tell but, when he wrapped his strong hands around me and gently picked me up, I knew we would both be satisfied within a few minutes.

I didn't care that our interaction took such a short period of time; the reason I existed was to appease him. We always captured snatched moments together; one of us with a hint of doubt and embarrassment, the other eager to totally surrender.

He tenderly laid me on the table and expertly opened me up - exposed for all to see. With one finger, he gently stroked me in places where plenty of people had been before. There had been so many that all their faces blurred into one. Only he mattered now; he was the one who needed me.

He looked at me, fleetingly up and down. He murmured something under his breath and then as he released a guttural cry of exclamation, I knew he was finished with me. I didn't feel used this time; I knew he'd be back for more.

He straightened me up, ensuring that nothing was out of place. He lifted me once more, placed me back on the shelf between A-D and I-L and he walked away.

Joe, by Ella Saye

As I hold my poorly son's hand, entwined through cot bars,
I've been thinking of you.
Almost ten, as we unpacked trunks, we found matching pyjamas,
a shared birthday, destined to be friends.

Then a few weeks later, when noisy footsteps came to get you
and roused us from sleep,
still their day but the middle of our night
we listened in interested silence
until we heard your sobs of grief.

Then a long time later you came back
because, well, where else could you go?

And night after night, we held hands,
across the gap between cold metal beds
as you sobbed silently.

And I think of your son, asleep across the hall.
Newly nine,
also an orphan.

Agnes, by Hannah Potter

It was a little after 7am when I reached her room. I knew she would be awake - she probably had been for a while now. I tapped gently on the door, and entered.

'Good morning, Agnes.

Good morning dear,' she smiled at me. 'What's your name?'

'It's me Agnes - Martha,' I reminded her gently.

Oh yes, of course... I could see the look of confusion on her face. The struggle behind her pale blue eyes as she tried to remember who I was.

'How did you sleep, Agnes?' I asked her, keeping my tone as light as I could.

'Oh, fine thank you dear, she replied.

'Really? No pain?'

'Oh, not really. Just the usual, you know.' She gave me another one of her lovely smiles. Agnes never would say if she was in pain.

I set her cup of tea on the table beside her bed.

'There you are, Agnes. Tea, two sugars.' Her eyes lit up.

'Ooh, thank you, dear. Are there any biscuits?'

Her child-like excitement when it came to biscuits always made me laugh. I usually managed to sneak her an extra one or two. Our secret.

'Of course,' I chuckled.

'Goodie,' she grinned. 'Is Charlie coming to see me today?'

I sighed. 'No, Agnes, not today.' Charlie, her husband, passed away years ago.

'Oh.' Her disappointment was tangible. I felt that familiar lump in my throat and fought back the tears. We go through this same thing every day. The same hope. The same disappointment. For months now.

'Shall I open the curtains, Agnes?' I ask quickly. 'The sun is out today, it's beautiful out there. How about a walk in the gardens later?'

'Yes, please. That would be lovely, dear.'

'I'll come by after lunch,' I promised her. 'We'll go around by the lake. See the birds on the water.'

That smile again. I can't wait!'

She stops me as I am about to leave the room.

'Excuse me, dear?'

'Yes, Agnes?'

'I was just wondering...what is your name?'

'Martha,' I say gently. 'My name is Martha.'

She nods. 'It's lovely to meet you, Martha,' she says warmly.

'It's lovely to meet you, too Agnes,' I tell her, before turning and leaving the room.

The Decision, by Sandy Calico

As Maggie drove home, on autopilot, she replayed the conversation with her mother.

'Mum, I'm not sure Phil and I will be together much longer.'

'You've only been married a few years, love. Phil's a good man.'
'He's boring me to death.'

There was something on the road ahead. She stopped the car. A male pheasant stood crestfallen, looking down at his mate, lying motionless.

Maggie, forlorn, stared with him.

She didn't want Phil to feel like that.

She reached for her mobile.

'Phil, we need to talk.'

The Lottery Win, by Nickie O'Hara

She sat on her faded, aged settee, clutching the crumpled lottery ticket, not daring to let it out of her sight. She'd chosen the numbers carefully – not the usual birthdays and anniversaries but numbers that she thought would be lucky. It was 7.30pm on a Saturday and the usual rituals of evening meal, washing up and the pouring of a glass of wine had been conducted. She was trying to stay calm but she always got jittery at the same time, every week. Her mind was full of 'What ifs...' and she almost couldn't bear the tension but she knew that was part of her enjoyment of the weekly ritual... or torture, whichever way you looked at it.

At 8.05pm the familiar theme tune struck up, the blue logo and the red writing to which she had become so accustomed flew into view on the television screen and she could feel the excitement and tension building.

As the host of the quiz show (used to pad out the 30-second draw into an hour-long show) appeared she tutted and shuffled in her chair. More time to wait! But she felt that she couldn't complain as the children enjoyed this bit, mainly because they had a one-in-four chance of getting the answer right thanks to the answers appearing on screen. And of course, they tolerated her little indulgence each week.

The crack of a can of lager opening to her right hand side made her jump slightly and she glanced over to her husband, sat in his usual chair, relaxing with his drink, waiting, uncomplainingly until the children had gone to bed, when they could snuggle together on the settee with a bootleg copy of a recent film from his 'hush-hush-wink-wink-say-no-more-it's-cheap' mate at work. The jolt back to reality prompted her to look around her cosy lounge and appreciate what she already had... a roof over her head, happy, well-fed children, a loving husband. But she had her dreams. She was allowed, wasn't she?

A drum roll pounded out of the speakers of the television, a pretty, young, blonde female presenter stepped in front of the camera and proceeded to speak to a bodiless voice known as 'The Voice of The Balls'. The usual banter about independent adjudicators and random machine selection took place and the weekly call of 'Sssssshhhhhh' reverberated around the lounge.

She checked her ticket one more time and then kept her eyes glued to the television screen.

The first ball dropped into view...
The second ball dropped into view...
The third, the fourth and the fifth...
Then the sixth...

She looked at her ticket. Her family turned and looked at her. She looked up and shook her head and they all heaved a sigh of relief.

Another week without a win. She'd proved, once again, that she didn't need to win the lottery to be happy and she tucked the two-year-old ticket back into her purse ready for the following week.

A Silent Place, by Penny Smith

My feet walk silently through the day,
soft-stepping over cracks and flaws.

The pavement slabs, dusty and grey.
make no echo as my sandals fall.

No sign remains to show I passed this way,
or even that my life's been lived at all.

The Answer Is No, by Penny Smith

No
stalling;
rhyme's calling,
begging my brain
to start work again
on yet another set
of rhyming couplets. So let
battle commence! Get brain in gear
choose words to make the enemy fear
the lash of tongue or mental cut and thrust
designed to conquer, though that be unjust
in what should be a friendly skirmish.
May each foray end as I wish
in compatible joining
of like with like, bringing
harmony to all.
forget the call
to arms. Smile!
Worthwhile,
No?

Two Sides to Every Story,
by Nickie O'Hara

brr... brr... brr... brr... brr

Bel stretched out her left arm and clicked the snooze button on the alarm clock. The morning sun brightened the room as it shone against the beige cotton curtains. She opened one eye and squinted at the digital display on the alarm clock. 06:40: she had 10 more minutes until the alarm rang again and she intended not to rise from the bed until the last possible second but already her mind was whirring with the list of tasks to be accomplished that day.

***

brr... brr... brr... brr... brr

Joe heard her alarm clock bleeping away and felt the slight movement in the bed as she stretched out her arm to hit the snooze button. Why did she do that? He knew that she was awake – her breathing was different. What was she thinking as she lay there? He felt himself drift... slowly... back... to... sleep...

***

brr... brr... brr... brr... brr

She turned in bed, opened both her eyes and looked at the digital display again although she already knew what it read. 06:50. Carefully and smoothly she swung her legs out of the bed, padded round the bedroom barefoot, collected the clothes she'd strategically piled on the dresser as she passed and made her way to the bathroom. On the way down the landing she called into each of her boy's bedrooms, waking them up, reminding them that it was a school day: 'Jamie! Ben! Time to get up. School. Now!' she called briskly.

She washed quickly and brushed her teeth, then dressed herself in the tiny bathroom so she wouldn't disturb Joe in the bedroom. She couldn't cope with his self-absorption this early in the morning. It suited her that he chose to stay in bed although she often wondered what would happen if she refused to get up in the morning.

She caught sight of her reflection as she pulled up her tights and looked away again quickly. No wonder he didn't want to touch her as often these days. She was three sizes bigger than when he'd met her twenty years ago, lumpy, saggy, scarred from operations; she poked at the excess flab on her thighs.

brr... brr... brr... brr... brr...

He felt the bed move as she reached to turn the alarm off and she climbed out of bed. He watched her through almost-closed eyes as she moved quietly around the bed, picking up clothes to wear in her usual smooth motion. 'I wish she wasn't so negative about herself' he thought. 'I wish she'd give me a chance. She's up first, to bed last, she always wears pyjamas. It's almost like she's avoiding me.' He could hear water splashing in the sink in the bathroom and the boys moving around their bedrooms. He rolled over onto his back and waited.

✳✳✳

It was Friday evening. Bel had rushed home from work, phoned up and ordered a take-away for everyone from the local Chinese, wishing that someone had already done all this considering they were having a rare night out together with friends; it was someone's birthday. A little while later, she stepped out of the shower and wrapped herself in a large bath towel then used a smaller one to rub the excess water from her hair. One look in the mirror told her it was going to take longer than the usual ten minutes to look presentable. She stepped closer to the mirror and pulled slightly at the delicate skin under her eyes, trying to stretch the brown shadows away. Grabbing the tweezers from her make-up bag she plucked away a few stray hairs from her eyebrows... then one from her chin... then a couple from her top lip... then gave up. She quickly applied her make-up and chose a dress from the wardrobe. After she'd put it on, she tugged at the material, wishing it would fit better. Squinting her eyes at her

21

reflection, she tried to imagine herself half a stone lighter. Yes, that would smooth the lumps and bumps if nothing else.

Shrugging at her reflection she attacked her hair half-heartedly with the straighteners, smoothed some wax through it, gave it a bit of a shake and tugged her fringe over her forehead and her non-existent wrinkles. She heard Joe's heavy footsteps coming up the stairs, shoved on her high-but-comfortable shoes and, as he walked into the room, she gave a little tip-toe twirl, 'Will I do, love?' She heard the response, 'You look fine', choked back the tears that welled up and headed out of the room to grab a tissue before she smudged her mascara. All she wanted was for him to really like the way she looked.

***

He watched her out of the corner of his eye as she flew through the front door at 5.15pm. Smoothly, and without pausing, she hung her coat on the rail, kicked off her shoes, picked up the phone, placed the regular Friday evening order at the local Chinese take-away and started organising the night's events, 'We're meeting Maddie and Steve at the pub at 7.30, then we'll probably do the usual route round town. Have you got your shirt sorted out?' She hardly took a breath and he felt she needed to slow down. He would offer to do a few things for her but he knew she would only brush him aside and profess that she could do them quicker on her own.

Whilst she was in the shower he got his shirt out of the wardrobe, gave it a quick shake and hung it up over the door. He stood sideways as he looked in the mirror and smoothed his t-shirt over his ever-increasing paunch, hoping that the shirt would still fit. As he heard the shower shut off, he grabbed his electric shaver and headed downstairs so she could use the bedroom in peace. After a quick spruce-up he headed back up the stairs and into the bedroom to get changed. He saw Bel and thought she looked lovely. After all these years, she still managed to look beautiful without going overboard; just gorgeous. 'Will I do, love?' she asked. He never knew how to pay her a compliment that wouldn't get brushed aside or that she wouldn't protest against and think that he was making it up to pacify her so he replied with, 'You look fine.' As she pushed past him he was aware he may have said the wrong thing, raised his eyes to the ceiling, opened his arms in silent despair and started to get dressed.

***

They stumbled through the front door just after 1am, both more drunk than they had been for a while, still laughing from the good night they'd had with their friends, giggling whilst sharing a memory from earlier.

Remembering that the children were away for the night they looked at each other and Bel glanced towards the stairs, 'Race ya...' she said, and set off up the stairs. Joe chased after her and they threw themselves on their bed, tearing at each other's clothes, kissing wildly. 'I love you so much,' murmured Bel. Joe slowed for a second and drank in those words. 'I love you too,' he whispered back. Bel could hardly believe what she was hearing but didn't question it and savoured the moment.

***

A short while later, Bel was curled up under the duvet, relishing the shared moments, wishing it was always like that. When she thought Joe was asleep, she slid carefully out of bed and padded to the bathroom, not bothering to put on her dressing gown, enjoying the naughtiness of being naked. She looked at herself in the mirror and cocked her head to the side. She didn't know whether it was the after-glow of sex but she decided that what she saw wasn't too bad after all...

***

Joe felt Bel slide out of the bed and watched her walk confidently towards the door. He thought back to only a short time ago when he'd been exploring every inch of her beautiful body. He couldn't wait for her to come back...

The First Casualty of War,
by Steven Herrick- Blake

They come ferreting through the bindweed
Dropping bobble hats and gloves in the rush;
A line of duffle coated warriors
Slogging over terrain rough as new landfill.

The cemetery erupts with the bold
Lung explosion of shrill voiced mortars
And invisible grenades. Right arms carried
Like automatics judder with school yard kick-back.

What foes there are drop by the thousand
But there are some who do not die easy.

Ranks of guanoed seraphim stand
Against the advance goading the crosshairs
To collect and dog them like midge flies.
One squaddie more astute in his brutality than the rest

Pistol-whips the neck of a submissive angel
With a club of wood. He is saving bullets.
There is a god shattering crack – real not voiced -
And every tongue stops.

What crows there are fester upward
And offer amused cat-calls to the air.

Some are too wise to the ways of death.

The Bigger Plan, by Caroline Finnerty

'He doesn't like you y'know,' my mother said.

'How the hell do you know? You've never even met him!'

'That's my point! Anyway I don't have to have met him, I can tell these things.'

'Oh and what are you now psychic?' I practically spat the words at her.

'No – but I can see it's you doing all the running.' *You doing all the running.* The internal monologue mimicked inside my head. God how I was sick of that bloody saying.

'What the hell do you know?' I stormed out of the kitchen full of 17-year old contempt and insolence and ran to where I was meeting him. We walked through the long grass with not much to say to each other.

I lay on my side so as not to take up too much space in the single bed where he lay flat on his back. My head was uncomfortable resting on his taut bicep but I didn't say anything.

'That was my first time y'know.'

I didn't need to be able to see his face to know that my announcement had come as a bit of a shock; I could feel his whole body instantly go rigid. Did he not know? I thought he would have known. Could he not tell? It wasn't what he wanted to hear; all the enthusiasm of the previous few minutes evaporated, leaving us lying in an awkward aftermath. Idiot! What did you go and say that for? Now you are really showing yourself for the schoolgirl that you are. The conversation changed then to stars and constellations and the universe as an infinite power which seemed a bit pointless because we couldn't see anything beyond the blue checked curtain. Was he trying to be romantic because it just felt... well, contrived.

The room seemed to be crowding in around us. The brown swirly carpet with orange flecks and the brown velvet curtains merged into one so it looked like the carpet was running up the wall or else the curtains were covering the floor; I wasn't sure which. The champagne coloured wallpaper had raised ridges that I wanted to pick at. Wasn't it the Super-Fresco range that was so popular in the eighties? Attention: can someone please tell the O'Brien household that we are now in 1997? It was a room full of patterns, clashes and ornaments; faux marble trophies sat in a cabinet beside porcelain figurines, china dogs and Victorian village scenes.

'Will you phone me?'

Silence fell on undertones of Catatonia's *Road Rage* playing on some late night music station.

'It's up to you boy, you're driving me crazy…'

'Thinking you may be losing your mind…'

'It's not over, it's not over, it's not over…'

His eyes didn't meet mine. I knew the answer.

'I'll write you a letter – haha!'

'Hahaha,' I laughed back, almost a bit too high. Do. Not. Cry. Don't you dare cry. Do not let him see you are upset.

'Open Your Eyes,' I shouted at him. Loud and strong, months of pent up rage finally being released.

But the words wouldn't leave my lips so stayed internalised instead. Why was he so blind to the fact that we were good together? Why didn't he like me? I wanted to be able to control how he felt. Maybe he would go away and miss me dreadfully and when he came back at the end of the summer we would pick up where we left off?

The long evenings finally came and the last few days of cramming for my Leaving Certificate exams were spent wallowing in Radiohead lyrics. I stared out of my bedroom window watching dust particles dancing in a beam of sunlight, desperately trying to come to terms with a broken heart and the Doppler Effect at the same time. The day I was starting my exams was the same day that he was leaving on a jet-plane to Boston with his college friends.

I took a job minding children while waiting on my exam results to know if I had got the university course I wanted. It was the same university that he attended. Tales would filter back through friends of friends of their wild stories that usually involved traffic cones, getting evicted by their landlord for throwing a house party and being arrested for drinking cans on the street. A world of freedom that I didn't yet have; it didn't sound like he was missing me.

***

Despite my early anguish; I got my happy-ever-after. He loves me and I love him with every inch of my being. As we watch our son grow together who would have thought all the hurt from earlier years would be forgotten as if it were never painless and just remains in memory instead? Those wounds from him have formed the person I am today, for the man who loves me today.

And I saw him the other day for the first time in eleven years in the queue at the supermarket; he had a small girl with him. Same clothes but with longer hair than the skin-head I last saw him with. He no longer had that same confidence of youth; the swagger or the appeal, he was ordinary. No longer special anymore; just like everyone else now. I looked away quickly, too afraid I might catch his eye, my head locked straight ahead in tunnel vision, not daring to look to the left or right. I had heard from a mutual friend that he had a daughter with a girl I once knew, they had got married; then they had a second daughter. He never used his degree, instead he turned his part-time job into a full-time one; one endless summer-job. They all live together in an annex built onto the side of his parents' three-bed semi-d, the one with the swirly carpet and Super-Fresco wallpaper. I heard that his wife is slowly going round the twist from having the in-laws next door.

In the glimpse that I caught of him the only thing I felt was relief. Glad that life didn't go the way that I had desperately wanted it to. Glad the future was out of my control. Glad I didn't get what I wished for. Sometimes life has a bigger plan.

The Bed Head, by Alison Percival

My parents never left us with relatives or grandparents or friends ever.

Apart from one time.

Once they left us with our step grandmother. That 'step' is quite important. I'm sure they must have told us beforehand that they were going to leave us whilst they went away – who knows where - but I remember it only dawning on me as I watched my father try and do a tricky three point turn out of her drive.

Don't worry, I'll look after you, said my big sister. I must have been younger than seven because my baby sister was not yet born.

My step grandmother was a curious woman, who wore her hair like a scalloped shell, like Wallis Simpson. And she was loathed by my mother as much as Wallis was loathed by the English for taking away their King. I can see her now, fag at the edge of lip, humping coal for the boiler. She had fallen out with her own sister over a tea set in a will. Her other relatives phoned in their performances. My Dad was the dutiful son to the last.

There was a story that she had survived on nothing but lemons for a while when she was a girl and the servants had found the peels in the incinerator bins in the grounds. It would have explained the sourness but that story doesn't square with the fact that my Grandpa married the housekeeper after the death of his beautiful elegant wife when my father was a young boy, and then died himself. The mother he was made to stare at in her casket on a bed of purple silk and to this day he cannot stand me wearing that colour and once made me change my dress.

She left us to our own devices that weekend. Everything was 'presently, presently' but presently never came.

She had a spinning wheel we played *Rumpelstiltskin* on or else *Sleeping Beauty*, (we had already cast the wicked Stepmother) and one of us would be the prince, hacking down the thorns. We coloured in doilies. She had a trio of Chinese rugs we would play stepping stones on, leaping from one to the next. One was Cree. The carpet was a sea of crocodiles. She had solitaire we played endlessly and a card table which swivelled and an ashtray in the shape of a monkey.

At night we slept together in a double bed with nylon sheets. The sheets were tucked so tight it was like getting into an envelope and we would lie like toy soldiers in a box, arms pinned to sides until one would help the other wriggle free. The static caused by our matching pyjamas made our hair stand on end. We put our heads under the sheets and watched the crackles. We hooked the sheets up and made a den. We pressed a torch to our fingers and looked at the red glow. And held the torch under our chins and did spooky laughs.

The headboard to the bed was made of a dark brown wood and the moulding looked exactly like squares of milk chocolate. When it was

29

night time and I cried for my parents, my sister broke off pieces and 'fed' me them. She whispered secrets to me in the dark.

***

When my sister died my step grandmother didn't come to the funeral because a) she thought it would be too upsetting and b) she was worried the boiler would have gone out by the time she returned.

When my step grandmother died, my father, being her son, inherited everything, although the other relatives tried to argue over the word 'step.'

I didn't want her monkey ashtray, or the silver ashtray that swivelled up, or the card table, or the drinks trolley which she would wheel in at exactly 6.30 for the first of her many Gordon's and Bitter Lemon of the night, or the owl on the stick in the garden, or the spinning wheel or the brooch with the Chinese man that had a little pearl on the end of his fishing rod, or the Willow Pattern plates, or Mr Salt and Mrs Pepper or the bowl she always made blackcurrant jelly in (no other flavour – ever) or the clock that had moulded beads going round which looked like Maltesers.

I would have liked that bed head though.

The relatives, toadies and humbugs one and all, came and took all the furniture, piled it all up and sold it.

Tales Out of School, by Jeannette Ellwood

What we want to see is the child in pursuit of knowledge and not knowledge in pursuit of the child.
George Bernard Shaw

I fell into the job almost by accident.

I had very recently qualified as a teacher at a time when there was a shortage of primary school teachers.

I did the fast track course as a mature student, came out with an English Hons. qualification – not very useful – and a teaching certificate, which got me an instant job.

My 'interview' was casual in the extreme. I heard through the village grapevine the Reception class teacher had just left and they needed a replacement, so I rang Mr W, the Head of the Village School.

'Come for a cup of tea this afternoon, about four. I will give you a tour of the school,' he said.

The large Victorian School building, a stone's throw from the graveyard and the church, was at the end of a blooming, heaven-scented, privet-hedge-lined drive.

The heavy studded front door, with its key still in the lock, was open to let in the late summer sunlight. Mr W, a shortish, pleasant looking man sporting a red bow tie, welcomed me on the doorstep.

'Hullo, you must be Mrs A. Do you like water colours?' he greeted me with a smile, and led me straight into his office where he had several paintings arranged on the floor, leaning against his chair, desk and wall.

'They are delightful,' I enthused. 'I especially like this one.' It was a soft sunset view of the Chiltern Hills.

'Yes,' he said 'that was done last year. I think it is the best…' he trailed off, obviously thinking deeply.

'Here,' he announced. 'Here,' and he lifted it and held it against the wall opposite his desk.' What do you think?'

'Great! Beautiful! You will be able to look at it while you work.' I replied.

'I paint watercolours. I am currently preparing for an Exhibition – in London,' he added with some pride.

He indicated I should sit and drink a cup of tea, resplendently served in beautiful porcelain cups and saucers.

Not the usual teacher-mug-with-a-brew I had become so used to.

'When we have finished I will show you your room.' He sipped his tea slowly, savouring its aroma.

'We are very old fashioned here, but don't worry, I hope to improve the facilities in the near future.' He gazed round his office, looking at each painting in turn.
'Hmm,' he murmured absently and beckoned me to follow him.

As he led me to the Reception classroom, through the hall, all I had time to observe was that the parquet flooring was slightly dusty and there was a large stove in the corner.

He opened the door to a high ceilinged, brick lined room, painted a very soft off-pink, which also housed an extremely black brute of a stove caged behind a wire mesh fire guard with an old fashioned brass rail along the top. It dominated the scene.

The small infant sized tables and chairs shrank to midget proportions in that setting. The teacher's desk was covered with a film of dust and the black oiled floor looked as if it could do with a good sanding down to its original oak splendour. He allowed me an extremely speedy glance round when I was then slightly pushed out of the way as he withdrew, closing the door softly behind us.

'Well that's it,' was all he said.

Back in his office, Mr W got out some papers and pushed them towards me.

'The bureaucrats have to be served, could you fill these in and bring them back with you when you start next week? Our first day of term is Tuesday.'

I was taken aback and asked feebly, 'Can you give me the job - just like that?'

He gave me a beatific smile, 'Oh yes,' he said. 'I don't believe in all these new rules. They hinder progress and cause too much red tape,' he went on. 'Would you like an envelope?' He handed me an extremely large one with *Dacorum Education Office*, already printed on the front.

'You can deal with all the formalities,' he instructed me. 'Make sure your references are in order and enclose details of your qualifications, I am sure we will work very well together.' He held out his hand, and stood up.

'You have fifteen children in the class, some very naughty boys and one or two really nice little girls. I am sure they will enjoy you as a teacher. I want everyone to be happy.'

We shook hands and he closed that formidable front door behind me. I heard the key turn in the lock. He was very eager to get back to his paintings.

As I walked home clutching the Education Office's envelope, I looked at the beauty of the surrounding hills. I could smell the hedgerow's aromatic perfume mix of hawthorn, *Rosa canina* and blackthorn. I got a smile from a couple of women I met walking along

Newground Road, towards the house I had recently moved into and I enjoyed the view of fields and trees as I walked.

But in spite of my love of the countryside, and the friendliness of the people, I thought: 'I am mad to even consider a job in an old fashioned dirty school, with an absent-minded eccentric Head and 'naughty' boys, whatever the word 'naughty' means. I would be wise to accept that job in Tring Primary School, with an up-to-the minute Headmistress and spotless classroom with all the modern equipment.'

I had already been warned by my tutor at University - and others - that whilst teaching in a village school environment offers unique opportunities, it requires a certain sort of person to cope with its idiosyncrasies.

'Aim for a good urban school,' he had advised. 'Take a further qualification and apply for headships when you have gained a little experience. A stint in a village school will not enhance your career prospects. Don't forget, it takes a certain sort of person to sink into country life.'

I looked at the envelope in my hand, I remembered the eccentric, amiable Head and thought of the children whose ancestors had lived in the village for generations, and made their mark there. I remembered the local paper saying that newcomers were changing the face of the countryside, perhaps I could help change the face of village education?

It would be a challenge. It would mean taking a chance. I felt a stirring of interest; it would be dreadful to miss an adventure…possibly even a life changing experience.

So, I jumped in with both feet forgetting my earlier aims of achieving a headship. I would embrace village life, glory in the beauty of Ashridge Forest and the surrounding Chiltern Hills, and relish the peculiarities of the present Head of that relic of Victoriana - the delightful rural school

Which is why I spent the next fifteen years or so living and working in the rich and heady mix of interesting, sometimes eccentric local people, leavened by newcomers, and teaching children who crept under my skin, into my life and remain in my memory forever.

This unique kaleidoscope of experience broadened my outlook, introduced me to people I would never have met in the anonymity of a town, and gave me an all too brief glimpse into a way of life that was passing before my eyes. I never found out whether I was that 'certain sort of person', my tutor had described to me, all I can say is that I wouldn't have missed those halcyon village school days, with its mixture of pain and tears, pleasure and laughter, for anything.

Unwelcome Break, by Alison Percival

We have been driving for five hours. The dogs are restless behind the grille.

Nearly there. You're going to love it. There's a waterfall. Wait 'til you see the waterfall, he says.

I really need this break. Bailiffs knocking on the door looking for the previous tenants, police ripping up carpets in the joint stairwell to reveal a layer of stolen credit cards, as thick as underlay, mine amongst them. A job that has turned from gold to dust. And a flatmate I am in love with who doesn't love me.

This man I am with, the man who is driving, is not the man I want. He is an escape route. Is that so wrong?

There will be mountain air. And stars at night.

I have a secret in my pocket. A note like your Mum wrote for you to get off games. A Get Out of Jail Free card. Signed off work. Three weeks.

***

I had imagined a man in a black polo neck, wearing little round glasses. Not this woman, only slightly older than me, tipping back in her chair.

Why can't you eat? she says, without stopping for an answer.

It's because you want to lose your curves and make your body androgynous so this man will desire you, isn't it?

Er, no, That's not it.

It is. You are in denial.

Okay then.

I don't go back.

***

We are still driving.

There's something I ought to tell you before we get there, he says. As an afterthought. *My ex will be there.*

Ex who? Ex wife?

No, we were never married. I'm sure I've mentioned her. When we split the houses, we couldn't decide who would get this one so we

36

share it. She lives there, most of the year. Unless I want it. She's a fantastic cook.

That's okay then. At least I won't starve. Although I am not eating much right now. It makes me gag.

He reaches into the glove compartment and gets out a box of travel sweets. I need anti-nausea ones, not barley sugars.

Couldn't you have chosen a weekend when she wasn't there?

We arrive. I see her in silhouette. As I crunch up the path, it is evidently news to her too.

So who's this? Younger than the last? And stepping out from behind her is a man, about the same age as me, peering out from shaggy black hair.

This - is Joe, she says, triumphantly. Beat that.

It is 4am. I am bone tired. My legs are cramped from sitting in the car. The Aga is on but it is unwelcoming. My boyfriend goes to get the bags out of the car and let the dogs out. By the way she greets the dogs, I realise they are shared too. Whilst he is gone she says, baring her teeth,

This is my kitchen. If you want anything, please ask me first.

There is only one double bed.

We should have it, he says. *I bought it.*

I bought the mattress. Don't you remember?

What use is a bed without the slats? You can sleep on the slats.

You never bought me anything.

You can have it.

Joe looks at me. I look at him.

We sleep squashed against a wall in a single.

The next morning my boyfriend is gone. I have no idea where. I stay in the bedroom. I'm too scared to go down to the kitchen. I look out of the window and see Joe talking to the cows in the field.

My boyfriend comes back. He has been gone hours.

A double bed is strapped to the roof-rack.

The First Meeting, by Carol Smith

Beth looked around the living room one more time, checking that everything was perfect. Today it had to be perfect. She was nervous; they hadn't seen each other in over a year and she wanted it to go well. She left the room and walked into the nursery and looked down at her son, sleeping peacefully. He looked just like him, had his eyes and nose and there was no denying that they were related. He had been so angry when he found she was pregnant; she remembered the arguments that had gone on for days. She had to leave; it was for the best. So sneaked out one day when he was at work.

Of course it wasn't easy to start off with: four months pregnant, no job and nowhere to live. Jane had taken her in until she found the small flat. She worked hard to make it liveable, all her money went on the nursery. She felt her eyes prick with tears and wiped them away; she kissed her son lightly on the forehead and quietly left the room, closing the door gently.

Beth plumped the cushions and then went to check on the cakes she'd made earlier. He had always told her that her cakes were the best. 'You could make a living from baking cakes,' he'd say, but she would always laugh it off. He would be so proud, she thought, when he found out that she was going to night classes and planning to start her own business. The door bell rang and her stomach flipped; she had a quick glance around and walked towards the door. Tears welled in her eyes as she opened the door. She had missed him so much, missed having him in her life.

'I'm so sorry Beth,' he said as he held out his arms. She fell into them and held on tight, her heart beating so fast that she could barely breathe. After what seemed like hours they let each other go and walked into the flat; he looked around and noticed how warm and homely it was; it had the 'Beth' touch he thought. They sat down on the sofa and just stared at each other.

'Can you ever forgive me Beth? I didn't mean to make you leave. It was just such a shock…'

'You're here now that's all that counts.'

Before they had the chance to say anything else, the baby woke up and started to cry.

'Would you like to meet him?' she asked.

He nodded. The moment they both stepped into the nursery he stopped crying. The baby looked up at them both and smiled. Beth picked him up and handed him over,

'Daniel, meet your Granddad.'

Christmas, by Jeannette Ellwood

While shepherds washed their socks by night,
All seated round the tub
A bar of sunlight soap came down
And they began to scrub.
St. Saviour's School, Lewisham SE13 - 1942

I had just qualified as a primary school teacher when I rashly agreed to be responsible for the important task of producing the nativity in our small village school.

Each year the children acted some Christmassy story in the Victorian hall with its ancient homemade stage complete with curtains hung specially for the occasion. The Vicar, all the local dignitaries, the Chairman and members of the governing body and most of the parents came. A local reporter plus his photographer, both of whom turned up every year, could be seen smoking in the back of the hall.

As a newcomer into the tightly knit local community, I was extremely anxious to make a good impression on everyone. It was the era of child led education, self-expression and the 'integrated day'. Ideally, all aspects of education were child led and managed, with the teacher simply acting as a facilitator.

Imbued with fervour and enthusiasm, I was determined I would show them my approach to education was modern and progressive. I set out to impress the audience with my brilliant teaching skills. My first obstacle to exhibiting my talents was 'Mary'.

My class had elected determined, self-willed precocious Jennifer to take the part. Nothing meek, mild or gentle about her! Her rival for attention, and class leadership, was Mark, a handsome, studious boy with a stubborn streak. Not your ideal Joseph from Mary's point of view. However, as I pointed out somewhat unsympathetically, when 'Mary' took me aside to protest, 'That's show biz for you. Sorry.'

A determined group of children from my class duly allocated the lesser parts. I was full of misgivings but I stuck to my guns - and my ideology- of a 'child led and managed' production and started rehearsals.

Our first scene was the Angel Gabriel visiting Mary. She was supposed to be meekly sitting at home waiting for the Message from 'on High'. Not her style, unfortunately.

'I want to wear my party dress,' announced Mary to all and sundry - 'it's pink with a standing-out skirt and spangles all over it. My mummy made it for me.'

'…Erm, that isn't really what Mary would be wearing – remember some of the pictures I showed you?' I remonstrated gently.

'I don't care,' came the reply. 'I am going to wear my ballet shoes too!' (Jennifer was an aficionado of the ballet as her mother was a dance teacher.)

I smiled sweetly, falsely, and mentally shrugged my shoulders. 'All right, Jennifer, if that really is your view of Mary's dress sense, I suppose that's your decision.' She gave me a darkling look as she made for the dressing room.

The children had set the stage, putting Wendy House chairs from our class round a table complete with an electric kettle minus its plug, and assorted mugs. Our classroom's potted palm, placed stage left, was doing duty as an olive tree, reminding Gabriel where he was to make his entrance.

We had rehearsed various lines of script over the previous few weeks. Admittedly it had changed with each rehearsal as the children merrily ad-libbed as the mood took them, but everyone seemed to know what they were going to say so the reasonably accurate bare bones of the story emerged as we went on.

Apparently, unknown to me, Mary had decided to do some housework while waiting for the Angel Gabriel, and turned up on the night with a bright yellow duster and a dustpan and broom, ready in the wings, raring to go on.

I have to say I was extremely nervous as I peeped alternately between the curtains and the door to the room where the actors were corralled, waiting to make their entrances. As per tradition, the hall was full.

To my horror the local Education Officer, who was renowned for her sarcastic remarks about anything she took exception to, sat beside the Chair of Governors. Jennifer's mother, grandmother and father were sitting in the front row with Mark's parents and older brothers immediately behind them. Everyone looked expectant, anticipating an evening to remember.

The school band run by our head teacher started the first carol. Everyone studied his or her carol sheets and more or less started singing. The curtains opened and Mary pirouetted onto the stage and stood poised for dramatic effect. The singing died away as the audience took in her full glory.

Tutu quivering, duster waving and dustpan in hand Mary commanded total attention. She smiled sweetly and turned to the nearest chair giving it a hearty rub with her duster.

'I'm doing the housework,' she announced. 'I know Mary's mummy would like a nice clean house for when visitors come.' As she picked up the kettle she turned to her mother in the front row.

'This hasn't got HOT water in it because my Teacher wouldn't let me plug it in, Joseph will have to have COLD tea. Tch! tch!' she waved it about dramatically and almost slammed it back onto the somewhat rickety table.

She proceeded to dust the mugs, taking out a teabag she had hidden down the front of her tutu. She put it into her favourite mug, with the cat motif.

'He's late again,' she said, arms akimbo, as we heard a tentative off-stage knock.

A figure appeared in what looked like a *Dunelm* dressing gown with wings from the local *Accessorize* shop sticking out the back.

'I didn't say 'Come in!' Anyway you aren't near the tree - go out and come in again.' hissed Mary

Gabriel looked sheepish, blushed and meekly turned back and re-emerged just behind the 'olive' tree stage left. He stood on one leg for some reason and spoke:

'I've got some good news for you…'

There was a long pause.

'…er tidings,' he looked at the crumpled bit of paper he had clutched in his hand. 'No… ti -d –ings of big happiness.' He stopped abruptly.

'Great joy,' came a voice from the back of the hall (his brother?).

Mary turned to the audience and said indignantly 'This is OUR Play, if you keep shouting like that you will PUT US OFF.'
The 'brother' looked suitably abashed.

'Yes?' she looked kindly at Gabriel, 'what else have you got to tell me?'

'You're pregnant – it's a boy – you will call him Jesus,' stammered Gabriel

Mary's kindly look disappeared in a flash. 'I TOLD you I don't like that name, remember I said Darren, I like DARREN.' She repeated it very loudly looking first at the hapless angel and then at the audience.

'DARREN!' she almost shouted. By this time, audience attention was breathlessly captured.

Utter silence prevailed.

The reporter from the local paper looked slightly stunned but the hall flashed like a disco with the photographer taking photos first of the stage then of various members of the audience – focussing I regret to say on the expression on the Education Officer's face.

For the first time the angel looked determined. 'You can't change his name. It's God's baby and what He says goes. Always!' he asserted. 'Anyway Teacher said it was already written in the Book, you know – that special Book, The Bible.'

I had some hopes he was remembering us all talking about God's omnipotence and omniscience. Maybe some of my words in RE had lodged somewhere.

He delivered his exit line, 'Remember, it's not Joseph's son, it's God's and he is jolly pleased with you for being so helpful…Goodbye.' He waved cheerfully at the audience and almost skipped off the stage obviously thrilled his bit was over. Mary muttered some words under her breath, which thankfully no one heard, and turned back to the table to pick up the kettle when Joseph unexpectedly appeared stage right.

He was resplendent in a striped kaftan with a *Homebase* stripey tea-towel on his head.

Mary eyed him with disfavour. 'What are you doing here it's too soon, I'm making tea and you're supposed to be carpentering until I've finished except that Miss has taken away the plug so I can't have hot water, only cold.' Resentfully she delivered her lines without pausing for breath.

'I know that,' said Joseph, nose in air 'I can't wait all day I've got customers to see to. I don't want tea anyway.'

Mary's colour rose. 'You can't change it all now, we agreed what to do. You've GOT to have tea. You're horrible. You've spoilt it. You're too stuck up anyway, aaand now - I really don't like you.'

'I'm your feeancee,' asserted Joseph, 'you have to like me, and you have to do what I tells you, it sez so in the Bible.' His carefully cultivated Received Pronunciation faded in the stress of the moment.

Mary dropped the duster she had been holding all this time and advanced threateningly on Joseph, who to give him credit, stood his ground. 'Oh no I don't, I'm not even married to you, and I wouldn't marry you anyway. You're bossy. Bossy boots, bossy boots,' she chanted.

'You've got summat to tell me,' he said stemming the flow, 'Remember the angel came to h'announce summat?'

Mary looked triumphant. 'Oh yes, he came. He's much nicer than you I'm going to marry him when I am 14.' She paused to see what effect that had on Joseph but he remained scornfully unimpressed. 'And anyway,' she went on, 'I'm in the club, and it's a boy, and I'm going to call it Darren NOT Jesus - AND what's more, it's not yours.' With that, she flounced off, stage-left, kicking the dustpan out of her way as she went.

There was stunned silence. The two children in charge of closing the curtains valiantly pulled on the ropes but they stuck half way giving the audience ample time to see Joseph walking quickly to the table and extracting the two chocolate biscuits Mary had hidden in one of the larger mugs in case of imminent starvation during her act.

The Nativity scene was to come next with lots of four and five year olds being either sheep or cherubs. Jennifer, deciding to be producer, had organised it entirely to her satisfaction...

The Angels sang, the shepherds did their bit; although there was one tense moment when Mary said her mum used Boots baby cream not myrrh for her baby. The newly arrived king, with his dangerously precarious crown, looked affronted at having his present sent back, but after a few words, the myrrh was allowed to join 'Frank's scents' and the gold, under the crib with real hay in it.

As the last carol echoed round the high ceiling of our lofty Victorian hall, the audience clapped and stamped (brothers again?) their appreciation. The Head came and gave me a tight reassuring hug as he wended his way hastily to the actors' noise ridden corral, and I died a thousand deaths hidden just behind the curtain.

I was waiting for Damocles, in the form of the Chairman of Governors, to drop his sword resoundingly on my head. Then amazingly, he stood up and shouted 'Bravo!' joining in with the rest of the audience. Mary's mother was fairly bursting with pride as the reporter rushed to her side for an exclusive interview.

Mary appeared, well in front of the curtain with Gabriel, and did quite a few pirouettes ending with a very creditable curtsey. The cherubs, lambs, Joseph and baby Jesus clutched in a Shepherd's arms stood well back. Her instructions I presumed. Fortunately, the rag doll that was Jesus didn't seem to object too much. The photographer rushed up to Mary and asked her to pose with Gabriel...

I was intending to slip away, but too late, the Education Officer asked to see the teacher who had been responsible for the entertainment.

'Well,' she said looking me up and down. 'Different...' she lingered over the word. 'Pity about the COLD water though... However, the rest was quite well done.'

At that, Mr Chairman turned to me, gave a wink with his off-side eye, took her arm and escorted her from the hall as she moved with queen-like dignity towards the exit pausing only to exchange a few words with the reporter from the local paper. They both turned to look at me, still standing there, rigid. I had a sudden mental vision of what the headlines might be – 'Virgin Mary in tutu calls Jesus "Darren" or 'Mary and Joseph Divorced over Angel Wrangle' or something like that. I gulped. Goodness knows what Mary did after her triumphant photo shoot; probably beat up Joseph for taking the chocolate biscuits when she wasn't looking.

As for me, I escaped on my bicycle under cover of the winter dusk, arriving home in time to pour myself a sizeable whiskey, turn on the TV and take the telephone off the hook. I would wait with bated breath to see the next day's headline.

Only two days until the end of my first term; I couldn't wait.

Poems from Atlantis, by Martin Burke

1

Sea-birds
Birds I do not know the names of
There at harbour and shore-line
A multiplicity brightening the day
Their waddling ways
A rightness equalling the rightness of evening
In which these lines are written

For their sake, for mine
For the little of beauty I know
For the given beauty of boats with names
As inviting as Island and Faros
Towards which they will soon be headed.

2

To make a painting is to make love to the wind
Is to make an occasion of grace from circumstance
To say to the future that the present existed.

So, as the wind curls in from the sea
I see that nothing changes and nothing will:

It is always the light which astounds us.

Kathleen Raine, by Martin Burke

"I couldn't claim that I have never felt the urge to explore evil, but
when
you descend into hell you have to be very careful."

To have kept the fire alive
Like a shield held up to the sun to bounce its rays back into the earth
Seeing the latent forest in the seed (call this my Scottish eye ye
disbelievers)

Some beginnings have no beginnings nor need one
Fire is old no matter how new
Being what I am I could never be what I was not

First love, then desolation –it is an old, an honourable, if outworn
story,
yet I have no other to tell

Or perhaps I seek a mirror which will not show me to myself?

In Blake I have found wisdom
In life few consolations

Yet to forgive oneself….I have not yet reached it -though the dead
continue
speaking to the living

Others have gone where I have gone –yet what footsteps can be
followed with
any certainty?
One spoke of a rose, one spoke of a garden
Perhaps I failed to follow but I did not fail to believe

Finding a language hidden within a language

Speaking….but that was later

Separating irony from paradox –and the roots of my hair sizzling!
Sweet water, sweet water, who but he did I ever marry?

If I made one mistake I made a second –yet is poetry not a suitable
recompense?

And under the water the calmness of deeper waters

Stirring old fires, holding a mirror up to the sun, holding a shield –
simple
gestures, but ah, the fullness of such simplicities

The pool that polished the stone I hold polished me also to this
nakedness
I would have no other for myself nor other to place before you

Remembering not to confuse, as AE said, 'the politics of time with the
politics of eternity'
Hence if I was the Hag I was also the Virgin –still am and will be even when
I am no more
The many traditions joining
The many traditions separating
(I have made my peace with such necessity)

Casting side-way glance into mirrors of water and ink

All my memories of Eden re-found in Scotland

Bright water, bright water, a timeless ink
The enduring ones –there in all I had forgotten (not Plato's dream but my
living truth)
Bright water and ink (do you begin to sense the calligraphy I trace out here?)

I held to my lover but he loved other than what I was
(No bright water now but the dark ink of pain)
Cursing him with an utterance no regret would repair
As if the Virgin bowed to the Hag and that act could not be undone

Undone, undone… the moon will undo me when it gives me a hundred months to
live
(I have even made my peace with this necessity)
As if merely to walk in the labyrinth of words was to find an unasked-for
redemption

Traditions joining, traditions separating, new wisdoms of an old alliance
The ink remade bright with fresh water
The labyrinth unwinding itself like a spool of thread to a straight path

Thus I come out of history into history

The cup I held out to my lover others now hold out to me

I drink bright water of a true tradition

Carve no other words upon my grave.

2

February. Unexpected snow. The great impertinence of beauty.
Sabbath of
hope, Sabbath
of love, bringing grace to the living, grace to the dead, grace to all
crafts sweetening
the air

Voices ring in my mind; I grow strange to myself but this is pleasing.
The
mind is addressed
by the thousand calling voices of the air –as if the genius of place
found a
voice I hear,
respond to, note and make a measurement of
This is what we long for – a work that is lifelong and longer, where
the
quietness of the heart
and the eye's clarity achieve a harmony that can be danced to under,
as
Neruda says,
an amber moon with amber shining in your heart

I reach the last stand in my going - but what are destinations to the
questioning mind when we
are always beginning? We seek the comfort of the sun, we seek the
comfort of
the
moon - but brother, nothing can equal the light in its scintillation

I have become what I have become; a man that would be simple and dreamless
amid the
luminous small new leaves unfolding, whose privilege in this unremembering
time
is the beauty and sorrow of trees

I see there the blatant purpose in the renounced light of morning: this is
what we are called to
in the right season, this is what moves the heart and mind with hands newly
come to
the immortal work of memory and celebration

As a volleys of swallow rose into the brightening air that had unearthly
power to please the
needs of heart and mind

The rayed imperial light sang in the leaves it made in human time

Now the remnant groves grow bright with praise even in the pale daylight
which is holy
although we knew it not

And I thought: this is the world we have set on fire as a singer sings
unseen in the Sabbath of
the trees and I praise the joyous rage that justifies his page and sing for
the commonwealth of peace.

Interviews with Fiona Shaw, by Martin Burke

1

Your future begins when you give up your past.

You stand in terrible nakedness as history changes.
You are looking for that intensity of life
Which is supposed to come the moment before death.

You begin from where you want to arrive
Moving towards what you hope will be clarity:

Death is assured – revelation is elusive:
You move between the shadows which they cast.

2

(Electra)
Play her with innocence but also with deliberate care.

What is not in the text must be in your heart
For there are revelations of which she knows nothing
But you –you must be aware of them:

Rituals of the tribe, rituals of grief,
The inducements of politics to interfere with the living
While castigating the dead.

The web of history you have escaped from
Is the web she must enter;
Another ritual of the tribe, another human grief.

You are drawn to her, you become her
Becoming what she has always been-
A mind on the borderline of tragedy and tradition
In a manner the Greeks and Irish understand.

This is the wasteland before the wasteland was written;
A landscape of nothing with a merciless sun
Under which other rituals must begin.

Who are we that we should find ourselves in her?
What cruel but necessary poetry forces such words
From her mouth in which there must be not repetition
Nor silence in experience, but revelation?

The play begins, the play ends,
We judge ourselves for what we are:
We have no masks to hide us from ourselves.

3

A restlessness which is an energy.
A question posing no immediate answer.
A history not your own becomes your own
Out of which you draw energy and resolve.

A Greek situation. Nothing you can rehearse
But must live to the opened rawness of a wound.

There is no stylisation of this condition.
The truth of one age slips into another in a guise
Which pleases that age

But the truths remain what they are
And you must find a persona for this condition.

How will you approach it?
How will you direct the play you are cast within?

The question frames, not an answer, but a condition.
Everything is pitched at the level of life before death.
You walk the tightrope between one and the other
Where are no answers given in advance.

A brother returns from death or a brother goes into death.
In both you must find joy and grief for the sisters they are:
Witnessing possibilities where light has not arrived.

Into dreaded dark we cast our hopes and human aspirations.

4

You enter a Greek amphitheatre and change.
You body is different, your voice-tone alters.

Imagination of course, but this is the site
Where imagination rooted in a lyric.

You are where you are in history and time
But you are also somewhere else.

You are older than the self you thought to be
Becoming the one in whose name you came
To this disquieting place.

History ripples, your spine shudders,
Shadows gather on the stage.

Life In the Corner, by 'Matthew'
(aka Neil Dickens)

About Me

I'm Matthew, I'm 6 years old. I have a Mum, a Dad and an annoying 4 year old sister, called 'Becca. I started writing this when I was two. I had more time on my hands in those days. Becca wasn't even born and I didn't have to attend school for every waking hour. Still, whenever I can I get up to mischief and I document my adventures here.

1. All I want for Christmas...

Yesterday's corner time: 6 Minutes.

Mum: 'Matthew, do you know what you would like for Christmas yet?'
Matthew: 'Yep.'

Mum: 'What?'

Matthew: 'A zombie.'

Mum. 'What?'

Matthew: 'A zombie.'

Mum: 'What? A toy zombie?'

Matthew: 'No, a real zombie.'

Mum: 'Isn't there a risk that it might eat you?'

Matthew: 'No, it will have a brain so that I can control it.'

Mum: 'I don't think that Santa's elves would like to make a zombie.'

Matthew: 'Really? How about a vampire then?

Mum: 'Hmm. Why don't you have a think about it.'

Mum: 'Dad, do you know what you would like for Christmas?'

Dad: 'Well, I think that may depend on what Matthew gets. Perhaps a large stake and some garlic.'

2. Music Group
Yesterday's corner time: 9 Minutes.
Dad took the morning off work and took Becca and me to music group.

Unfortunately, I think I may have ruined any chances that I may have had of receiving some Christmas presents this year after I attacked Father Christmas.

Actually, it wasn't really Father Christmas at all but a man dressed up to look like him. My suspicions were first aroused when he was unable to name all of Santa's reindeers but they were most definitely confirmed when his beard fell off.

'Hey! It's not really Father Christmas! It's, it's an impostor. Everybody, get him!' screamed my Dad.

I didn't need inviting twice. In fact, I don't normally need inviting once but it always helps.

Later on, in a reflective mood, Dad explained how it's deemed socially unacceptable to do what we did unless you're a professional wrestler. And even then, it's still only acceptable if actually in a wrestling match at the time.

Apparently, it's completely unacceptable to do what Becca did, even if you're a wrestler in a wrestling match. I'm not sure if I'll ever get the hang of social etiquette.

Also, I've noticed that my Dad always saves the most important snippets of information until it's too late. Had he shared this with me at the time, then perhaps we wouldn't all be barred from music group.

Dad and I have a two month suspension and Becca has received a lifetime ban.

Matthew.

3. Ears
Yesterday's corner time: 2 Minutes.

Someone once said that I was very advanced for my ears.

Naturally, I had misheard them but for quite some time, I had concerns that my ears were holding me back and preventing me from realising my full potential.

I would catch glimpses of my reflection in shop windows and wish that I had different ears. Why couldn't they be more like my other features, such as my nose, eyes or mouth?

My little sister Becca didn't help my paranoia.

No one had ever accused Becca of being very advanced for her ears. In fact, quite the opposite. People often commented how her ears should really be pinned back before they caused a serious accident.

That was shortly after one ear had carelessly flopped into the road resulting in a twenty mile tail back and aeroplanes having to be re-routed to Paris.

In church, her ears were greeted with awe and wonderment as the congregation exclaimed 'Jesus! Look at the size of those!'

Matthew.

4. Homework
Yesterday's corner time: 5 Minutes.

Apparently, it's not enough that I go to school everyday. My teachers, in their infinite wisdom, still deem my work/life balance to be out of kilter.

With a view to remedying this horrendous aberration, they are now sending work home with me. Work is crossing the threshold into my domain where play and relaxation are the only laws. Well, together with cleaning my teeth after meals, keeping my bedroom tidy and no inappropriate nudity but the less said about that the better.

So, instead of spending quality relaxation time in a trance induced state whilst watching TV or reaching the third level of zen meditation whilst massacring zombies on my DS, I am obliged to do Mathematics.

Twenty equations including division and multiplication. Not only that but they say to show your working. Show you're working? Of course I'm working, I don't have time for anything else.

What do they want – video evidence? Do they want a film of me sleeping too so they can see the difference? Here's one of Matthew working and here's one of Matthew collapsed over the table utterly exhausted.

Dad turned a ghostly pale when I mentioned that I was taking the video camera to school and he rushed off to wipe it.

So, at least it should be nice and shiny.

Matthew.

5. Slang
Yesterday's corner time: 8 Minutes.

Isn't school wonderful?

According to Dad, as an establishment for shaping young minds, it is probably only a close second to a young offenders institution. So, based upon that, I assume that it must be very good indeed.

The last few months have been very productive. I have been studying very hard and can now confidently say, that I am almost fluent in slang.

I think both my parents are pleased with my progress and visit the school's head teacher frequently to thank her. They were there again this morning prompted by my praise for Mum's large knockers. I thought this demonstrated nicely my sensitive and caring side.

I have also learnt that when someone kindly offers you a swift blow to your knackers that it is an offer that is best declined.

Unfortunately, I had to learn that one the hard way.

Matthew

The Good Samaritan, by Susan K. Mann

I slumped against the door, feeling my head swim with and trying to slow my breathing down. When at last I opened my eyes I was still in the busy waiting room; people were staring. I had no idea where to go or what to do, but I needed to get out as quickly as I could. The air outside the surgery was cool, like diving into water.

The office was the last place I wanted to go. They knew about the headaches; some knew I'd had an appointment and would want to know how I'd got on. A feeling of suffocation surrounded me and doubled me over, I grabbed a lamppost to steady myself before I crashed into the ground.

'Are you okay?' someone asked.

'Yes, thanks, just felt a bit dizzy. It's passing.'

'If you're sure you're okay. I can get you something to drink or eat if that would help?' He touched my shoulder and frowned.

Now he was just getting annoying. Leave me alone, I thought. I want to be left alone!

'I'm okay, but thanks.' I struggled to my feet in an effort to convince him and he made to walk away, but then looked back.

'Bye! and – thanks,' I said, meaning it.

I struggled on until I reached the sweet shop on the corner. Yes - a sugar rush; that's what I need. I knew it wouldn't really help, but I was in no position to resist. Jenning's was one of the few remaining shops that sold loose sweets stored in big glass jars. You know the ones I mean. You used to ask for quarters which came in little paper bags. Now with the metric system you have to ask for grams, which isn't right.

As usual I wasn't looking where I was going; too busy trying to concentrating hard on trying to look normal. And there he was again.

The Good Samaritan. Pitying.

'Sorry, I...'

Sorry I what? Sorry I look like this? Sorry I don't feel like talking?
Sorry for breathing?

'Let me buy those,' the guy said passing a handful of coins to the
woman behind the counter.

His hand brushed the hair out of his eyes as he took the change.

'I could've done that,' I said. 'I have got money.'

And then he smiled.

My head swam again and I felt the swirling, rolling sea-sickness
motion returning.

'Are you, you know, ok?' he said, never taking his eyes off me.

'Fine, but I'll pass on the sweets, thanks. I shouldn't be eating then
anyway.'

'Why, surely you're not worried about your figure? You look
fantastic.'

'Thanks.' I said, my cheeks burning.

'Would you like to go for some cake or a drink somewhere? My treat,
since I seem to have bought the wrong sweets.'

'Er, thanks. That would be lovely.' It was the easiest thing to say. I
felt so tired I wasn't sure that I could make it home anyway. I don't
normally do that kind of thing. But then, I don't normally have a
morning like this one. Who does? Well, everyone of course -
eventually. Why me? Why now? Why not. There's nothing like a bit
of bad news to concentrate the mind. And why stop at one drink?
What had I got to lose?

As we walked out of the shop, I thought I'd better give him another chance to leave.

'You don't have to do this, you know?' I was crossing my fingers that he wouldn't back out.

'I know I don't. I want to. Plus I need a sugar fix.' He said. I smiled to myself, a guy after my own heart.

We went into the first coffee shop we saw. We sat at a table in the window, the rare autumn sunshine seeping through the open blinds. The coffee shop was pretty empty and quiet; it was mid afternoon, so between lunchtime rush and the evening caffeine addicts.

'What would you like... er? I don't even know your name?' The guy said with a smile.

'It's Victoria, Victoria Sanchez or Tori for short. You?' I was running through a list of names in my head, trying to guess what suited him. Anthony, Luis...

'Dave, Dave Jackson. It's nice to meet you.' He extended his hand, which I then shook rather awkwardly. Dave, I didn't guess that one; it was so ordinary, when I didn't think he was an ordinary guy. I liked it.

'What can I get you?' He said again snapping me out of my daydream.

'Mmm... cola and a muffin, please?'
'Sure, back in a sex... I mean sec.'

Sitting alone, the memories of what I'd just heard came flooding back. I had been so distracted by meeting Dave, I had forgotten all about my appointment. Well, maybe not forgotten, but I had certainly put it to the back of my mind for the last twenty minutes or so.

Dave returned with a tray.

'Handy that,' he said. 'You asked for my faves too.'

'Oh, you love cola and muffins too.' I smiled trying not to be distracted.

'So...tell me something about you,' Dave said.

He was probably trying to be friendly, but it made me feel like I was being put on the spot. This was ridiculous; I was behaving like a fifteen-year-old. And time – my time, the time I had left – was marching on. I grabbed my bag and made to go but nothing happened. Or rather, it did. But not the thing I wanted. Where was I? Who was I? He was asking me these questions and I didn't know the answer anymore.

'Umm... I work as a computer support engineer. I have my own flat, not far from here. I have no family close by, and... well that's about it. What about you?' I left out the most important and most recent facts but then, I had just met the guy. I liked him and I didn't want to ruin it.

'Where do I start...? I work as a systems analyst, so I'm a computer geek like you.'

He smiled, to which I returned. 'I live with two flat mates, who are my best buddies. I have a younger brother and sister. Both still live at home with my parents, about 20 minutes drive from here. Anything else you want to know?'

'Everything,' I said aloud, without thinking. My cheeks flushed and Dave laughed.

'Ok, that might take longer than a cola and a muffin. What are you doing tonight?'
It took me back a little.

'No plans as such. You?' I said nonchalantly.

64

'Fancy dinner? I know this nice Italian place a few streets from here. If you like Italian food that is, or we can go somewhere else?'

'That would be lovely, I love Italian.'

I liked him, but inside my head was a voice screaming - what are you doing, do you really want to be getting involved with someone? Shut up, I'm going to have some fun before... I couldn't even finish off that sentence in my head.

'Maybe I should pick you up? About seven?'

Oh why bother. Why not just grab him now, here, and well.... I felt my cheeks reddening.

'Oh... is that too forward. Sorry.'

'No, that's fine,' I said. 'In fact, it's nearly six o'clock now. Why don't you...' come on round to my place, lock the door, take off that silly tie and...

'Ok, yeah...'

Too keen? Oh God, what was I doing?

We made a move.

'My flat is about ten minutes walk away, is that okay?'

'Yes, I have legs and don't mind using them,' Dave replied, making me giggle like a schoolgirl. We walked along the street, I tripped over something, I don't know what. I was oblivious to anyone or anything we passed, and I was so engrossed in Dave. Our hands brushed together, I felt the electricity between us. I know this sounds corny, but I felt like I was falling in love. God, I only met the guy about one hour ago, how is that possible? Maybe it was lust, maybe I was just confused, maybe I was just trying to escape. I swear I saw sparks when our hands touched. The next time they brushed together, our fingers interlinked, and then slowly we were holding hands, our shoulders touching as we walked. It felt right, it felt comfortable, and I think this is love. I thought to myself, but having never really been in actual love, I had nothing to compare it to.

'I live in this next street,' I said breaking the silence between us, which had not been uncomfortable at all.

'Are you allergic to cats?' I asked.

'No, why do you have one? I love cats.' My kind of guy.

'Yes, you'll love her.' I couldn't hide my big grin; he was perfect. From what had started as the worst day or my life, was starting to get considerably better.

'Here we are. I'm on the third floor.'

We walked up the stairs still holding hands. I felt sad when I had to let go of his hand to get my key from my bag. I opened the door and my cat, Midnight came padding towards us. She instantly took a liking to Dave and slinked around his ankles.

'Come in. Excuse the mess. I left in a hurry this morning. You've already met Midnight,' I said pointing at his feet, where the cat was still curling around him.

'Your flat looks great and Midnight is very friendly.' Dave was looking around while he spoke.

'Come in; make yourself comfortable.' Dave sat on the sofa, while Midnight jumped on his lap.

'Get down!' I said to the cat. 'Sorry - she isn't normally like that, she is usually hides under the bed when I have visitors.'

'She's fine. Like I said I love cats.' He tickled her under the chin and I could hear her purr with delight.

'Would you like a drink?'

'Er, yeah - great.'

I grabbed a couple of cans from the fridge but in my haste they crashed to the floor and fizzed over the tile. The bubbles oozed like brains as I clutched my head, digging my fingernails in my temples. Dave came running through and put his arms around me.

'Sorry about that,' I said. 'I've a bit of a headache.'

'Looked like more than just a headache.'

'I'm fine. I'm sorry.'

Dave's head came down to my level; he was nose to nose with me, snapping me back from my wandering mind. We gazed into each other's eyes for what seemed like an eternity. Automatically, my head tilted to the right and his to the left, we closed the gap between us and began to kiss. Hard and fast.

Next thing I knew he had me pinned up against the refrigerator. Our kisses became more intense, we moved through the living room, continually kissing and leaving a trail of clothes from the kitchen to my bedroom door.

I groped around for the door handle and flung the door open, while kissing Dave fiercely. Standing in my bedroom, in his Calvin Klein's, was a man I'd known for barely half a day. It felt like half a lifetime. What am I saying? It was half a lifetime: half my remaining life-time. My knees hit the bottom of my bed; I fell backwards and Dave was standing above me looking down, admiring what he saw.

Slowly, he lay down on top of me, removing my bra, kissing me all the way down until he reached my pants before removing them and kissing down the insides of my thighs.

After, when things had cooled, Dave pulled the duvet up as I began to shiver. I thought I must be dreaming. Did I really say 'I love you'? I sensed him smiling down at me. Did I imagine him replying, 'And I love you too. I've never felt this way before.'

When I woke it was four-thirty in the morning. I jumped up and turned round, convinced the space beside me would be empty. Once my head stopped spinning I could see the gentle rise and fall of his breathing. Running my fingers down his spine as he lay sleeping I said, 'Marry me?' Once it was out, I knew it was what I wanted more than anything in the world. Was I insane?

'What?'

'Oh God, I thought you were asleep.'

'And I thought I was dreaming.'

I held my breath. 'Well I mean, you're not a murderer or I would be dead by now - you've had plenty of opportunities.'

He laughed. 'What the hell, yes, yes I will marry you.' He reached up, cupped my face in his hands, and pulled me in for a deep, passionate kiss. We made love again and lay on the bed until the sunlight came cascading through the bedroom curtains.

'I suppose I'd better get a ring or something?' Dave said after lying quiet for a while.
'I asked you, remember?'

'This is madness, what will our friends and families say?' He sounded worried.

'Well, I only have my mum and this is our decision. Real friends will support whatever we do. What about your family?' I was beginning to think Dave was having second thoughts.

'I'm not sure; I don't normally do things on a whim. I'm not a spontaneous type of guy.'

'What if we didn't tell them, what if we got married on our own with a two witnesses off the street on say, next Monday?' I heard myself say.

'What? What's the big rush? You're crazy. Is there something you are not telling me? Are you pregnant or something and looking for a baby daddy?' Dave was sitting upright, looking at me accusingly.

'There is nothing, it's just I have waited my whole life to meet you and now I have, why wait?' I meant what I said. I think.

I was waiting for his answer; he was looking at me, as if he was looking for some other answer.

'Are you sick? Do you need a kidney or something, is that why you want me to marry you? If it were, I would give you what you needed without you having to get married. Come on Tori, tell me the truth. If you want me to marry you on Monday week I will, but you have to tell me the truth.' Dave held me by the shoulders looking me straight in the eye, I looked away. I had to tell him, didn't I?

'Life's too short. I have waited twenty-nine years to meet a guy like you, why wait any longer.' I said, not quite meeting his gaze.

He didn't speak for what seemed like an eternity. I stared at him, willing him to break the silence.

'OK, let's do it. Let's get married as soon as we can. I'll call work and take some holidays. Let's do this.'

'Ok, what do we need to do? I need to call my family? Do we need to book somewhere or register or something?' Dave said excitedly.

'I don't know. I have never booked a wedding before.'

'Is that not a gene women are born with?' Dave said sarcastically. I hit him with a cushion, rather than dignifying it with a response.

'We are really doing this?' I asked amazed.
'Yes, we are,' Dave said giving me a warm hug, which reassured me.

'I suppose I should call my mum,' I said, a bit reluctant.

'I'll call my parents, then my bro and sis.'

I found the perfect dress: a long, floaty, chiffon number with silk underskirt, the top a bodice style which tied up the back.

'We're on our own,' Dave told me coming off the 'phone. 'We'll get some witnesses there, anyone.'

'I know,' I whispered.

The night before I went to bed exhausted. I was so excited; I laid my dress out in the spare room, ready for the morning. I had been living in a bubble of romance for the past few weeks and I did not intend to burst it.

I woke early, ate some breakfast, showered and did my hair and makeup. I put on my dress, tiara and looked in the mirror. Getting in the taxi, I said to the driver, 'Take me to my destiny.' Corny, I know, but…

'What? Where's that?' the taxi driver asked confused.

I laughed. I was so happy. I walked up the steps to the registry office, my dress floating out behind me. I was aware of people in the street staring at me and I smiled, loving every minute of it. This was my moment.

Dave was inside waiting for me. He took my breath away as soon as I laid eyes on him. He had on a black tuxedo and looked like the next James Bond. I felt like the luckiest girl alive.
He smiled as I walked up to him. 'You look stunning.'

'Thank you, you don't look so bad yourself.'

'Are you both ready?' The registrar said.
We both nodded and followed her into the most beautiful room I have ever seen. There were no lights on, only pillar candles twinkling, casting shadows over the voile material draped along the ground to make an aisle. Tall vases with the most beautiful blood red roses I

have ever seen were everywhere. The altar itself had a balloon arch of red and white, in the shape of a heart.

The registrar turned to see the awe in my face and said, 'You are a very lucky woman for your fiancé to go to this much trouble.'

I looked at Dave. 'You did all this for me?' I couldn't believe it. 'Let's get married,' Dave said taking me by the hand and leading me down the aisle.

We got to the arch, turned to face each other and smiled. We took each other's hands instinctively.

The registrar started her speech. 'Do you Dave ... take Victoria Sanchez to be ....'

A seething pain seared through my head, I clutched at it. 'NO, NOT NOW' I yelled.

'Are you okay?' the registrar said.

'Does she look okay?' Dave snapped.

'I am fine, carry on,' I managed to gasp. Nothing was going to stop me from getting married.

She carried on, Dave said, 'I do' at his part. It was my turn, just before I was due to say, 'I do,' I collapsed to the ground. The pain was consuming.

Dave was on his knees beside me. My head cradled in his lap. The registrar above me, saying something I couldn't make out. I couldn't hear from the heartbeat in my ears.

I managed to say, 'I do' weakly. 'Please carry on, I need to carry on.' Dave's tears were falling onto my cheek, I could feel them, but I couldn't move my arms up to wipe them away. I stared into his eyes.

'I'm sorry.' I was crying.

Dave looked up at the registrar. 'Can you carry on please? I want Tori to be my wife.'

'Are you sure? Shouldn't we call an ambulance or something?' She asked.

'NO!' I shouted. 'I will not die in a hospital. Please carry on with the vows.'

Everything around me was starting to look hazy, with the exception of Dave's face. He looked like an angel with candle light glowing all around him.

The registrar speeded through the vows. Dave slipped the ring onto my finger.

'I now pronounce you man and wife,' the Registrar intoned. 'You may kiss the bride.'

Dave kissed me so hard it was all I that I could feel. The pain eased, my breathing slowed. I didn't want it to end, but everything has to come to an end at some point. Right?

Blue lights flashed angrily outside the Register Office window. My transport had arrived.

1

'So, world – here I am!'

No, don't be silly; I can't possibly start like that. I can't possibly begin my first blog-post in such a corny, unimaginative way. Ok, so how *do* I begin? What can I say that will get people reading? How to make myself stand out from the blogging crowd? Hmmm. Not as easy as you think, this blogging lark. I know; I've got it! I'll start by writing something funny. Yes – I'll tell a funny story. Ok, then. Funny. Here we go.

Monday 3rd July – Supermarket Sweep

You know how it is, you're in the supermarket and you're steering the trolley carefully, narrowly avoiding all the grannies chatting to each other right across the aisle; you steer a precise course down the centre, equidistant from each shelf, because if you didn't your little one would be stretching out his arms and reaching out for all those tempting-looking jars and cans. And you'll be half-way down the aisle before you realise the shelves are being emptied and that trail of devastation - those smashing bottles and those tins of baked-beans bouncing – is all your doing. Well, not strictly speaking yours – his: that cute, blue-eyed, blond-haired little cherub who is even now beaming like the very sun at all the people running round with mops and brushes and melting the hearts of all the pensioners tut-tutting at his mum. You know what I'm talking about, don't you? No? Well in that case this is probably not the blog for you.

Is it just me, or do all parents go through such public traumas when they try to go about their daily business? I need to know; that's why I'm sharing this with you. If you're a mum like me and you're as harassed as I am, let's commiserate. If you're not, if you're a super-mum and things like this don't happen, then I want to know your secret.

And if you're not a mum at all, go find yourself another blog to read (lol)! Back soon!

Yes, that's perfect. I like that, I like that lots. It sets up just the right light-hearted tone whilst at the same time making it clear what I'm about, and why I'm here. Of course, they don't know the real reason do they? Why should they? Let's just leave it there for now, shall we? Hit 'Publish Post' and see what happens. Ok then? Here goes!

Success! Your post has now been published. If you want to read it, click here.

I suppose I'd better have a look at it, just to make sure.

2

Oh – my – God. I mean, oh – my – f**king – God. Just look at the number of comments she gets! Forty-five! Forty-fucking-five for that wet fart of a blog-post. I don't believe you morons, really I don't. I mean – look! Look at *Supermarket Sweep* - quality writing; entertaining; educating. And what does it get? Three comments and a bit of Swedish porn-spam. My God in Heaven, where's the justice?

Of course, they all feel sorry for *her* don't they? 'Course they do. I mean, just look at some of the drivel they've written in the comments section:

Here's (((((Hugs)))))) honey, hoping you'll feel better soon.

You said that yesterday, roughly at the same time, luvvie...

Aw, poor you! You must be really suffering xxxxx

Xxxx? Spider kisses.

What's up kid? Sending you some positive Twitter vibes...

What's up kid? What's up? She's made that abundantly clear, you arse-hole – she's a self-centred, hypochondriacal attention-seeking and manipulating BITCH - 'sweetie'! Well, at least you got the 'kid' bit right - she is; and a bloody big one too.

Oh, stop bitching Gina. It'll do no good. And anyway, there's a pile of washing that you should be doing. Chances are at this rate it'll still be here when he gets home from work.

And of course, he doesn't understand what I'm doing blogging, does he? No. He'll come back home from work and take one look at the overflowing washing basket, sigh a bit and ask me: 'busy day, love?'

Then he'll start to load the washer, probably telling me to go and put my feet up, have a cup of tea, relax. Then after he's bathed Benjy, read him a story and put him to bed he'll probably offer to make supper. Oh God, why can't he just shout at me? Why doesn't he call me a lazy good-for-nothing, sponging off him, doing nothing all day but a bit of silly blogging? It's what I am, after all. And what I do. Why doesn't he hate me? God, I'd have some fabulous posts to write if he did.

3

'Hi honey…'

'I'm in here, on the sofa.'

'Hi gorgeous!' he calls. I offer him my cheek. 'Where's Benjamin?'

'Still napping. He's been upstairs for the last hour and-a-half.'

'And you've been blogging, I see. Let me have a look.'

And he takes the lap-top and sits down.

'This is good. I like this one,' he tells me. I'm not listening.

'I think I'll give up blogging,' I'm telling him. 'No, really. I'm through with it.'

'Really?'

'Really. I mean, what's it for? No-one ever reads this stuff.'
'I read it.'

'You don't count. I mean none of the others read it.'

'The others?'

'The mummy-bloggers, the inner circle, the big cheese bloggers with their groups and conferences and PR pitches.'

'Ah, the *cyber mummies*.'

And I have to laugh. Even though I want to cry.

'Don't you sometimes get that feeling, just occasionally, every now and then?'

'Not often.'

'Don't you sometimes want to throw the whole thing out, chuck it in, give it up completely and go into the country and just, I don't know, hug a tree or something? I do. Sometimes I really don't know where the next blog post's coming from; sometimes I really don't think I can match the quality blogs I'm reading; sometimes I just don't want to be a blogger any more.'

'Then what happens?'

'Oh, I don't know; I get an idea; something happens. Or I get an email; someone offering me something.'

'Ah...'

'Yes, *ah...*'

'And you realise it's actually quite lucrative.'
'I suppose it is, yes. I do.'
'And so you sit down at your lap-top and you tap-tap-tap away, and before you know it, you've got another post written and the comments start to come in and the whole cycle starts all over again.'
'Put like that, I suppose it does.'

'Of course it does. But it doesn't have to. It's really got to you, this blogging lark, hasn't it? You're an addict. You can't live without it.'

'No I'm not. I could give it up right now...'

'But you can't. Or you won't. It amounts to the same thing.'

'It doesn't.'

'What it boils down to is you keep thinking about chucking it all in but you never do. And never will.'

I say nothing; never do. Instead, I turn my back on him and get the lap-top out. After all, there are comments to be written on the posts that I've been reading. That's the way I'm going. If they won't come to me, I'll go to them, join in. I'll comment on everything they're saying until curiosity gets the better of them all and they come looking for me, commenting on my posts. Now, where was I? Ah yes, this post:

> They don't realise how hard it is for me. I feel so tired all the time. It's so depressing and I feel like I'm missing out on all the fun that Kylie and her mum should both be having.

Now if I just scroll down to the final comment. Yes, there it is again. I've found it:
> What's up kid? Sending you some positive Twitter vibes...

Do you want to add a comment? Do I want to add a comment! Silly question. Of course I do. So click 'Add Comment'. Here we go.

*Aw, hun, it must be awful for you. Here's sending you some
cyber-love. I'm thinking of you. Love, Online Mum of One*

That's it! Hit -'Send'.

APPENDIX

A Creative Writing e-course

Unit One: Getting the Habit

In this unit we'll look at getting, recording and developing writing ideas. We'll discuss ways of adapting the unnatural business of writing to our normal ways of thinking in order to get the most out of moments of inspiration.

Introduction

Writing is something we all do, everyday. Whether it's shopping lists, blog-posts, poetry or accumulating chapters of the next great novel, we're all at it. And it's amazing how many people *want* to do it: more often, for longer, for money, for pleasure.

Whatever your motivation – and whatever style or genre you're most interested in – I hope this course helps you take a few more steps towards achieving your goal.

Exercise 1.1
Before going any further, it would be worth considering for a moment what your personal writing goals are. What do you hope to achieve, and what do you hope to have gained by the end of this course?

A Brief History of Shopping Lists

Writing is actually quite an unnatural activity. Going back to shopping lists for a moment, the earliest examples of the 'written' word are actually just that – or more precisely, the lists made by ancient Babylonian merchants. The cuneiform tablets on which they kept tally of their stock are thought to be the first examples anywhere of the written word, so the next time you're writing a shopping list, remember that you're writing a little bit of history!

Human beings, though, have been around a good deal longer than the seven thousand or so years since the birth of writing. In evolutionary terms our brains haven't yet adapted to the written word, certainly not as written in neat lines on pieces of crisp, white paper. Yet so much of what we do depends on words, and an ability to manipulate them successfully is counted pretty universally as a measure of intelligence.

But our ideas don't tend to organise themselves in tidy sentences, nor in a logical sequence; still less do they lend themselves to being written down. This is why, sometimes, ideas that seem so brilliant in your head can look so disappointing when you see them on the page. And this, more than anything else, is the hard work of creative writing. If your bright idea is the one per cent inspiration, transferring it successfully to paper is definitely ninety-nine per cent perspiration. Thanks for that equation, Einstein!

That, then, is going to be the main business of this writing course: making the best of your ideas and improving your ability to communicate successfully with the reader. But I suppose we should at least start by considering where ideas come from in the first place. Staring at an empty sheet of paper or a blank computer screen is seldom very productive, so to begin with let's try something different.

Think of an event in your life that you can recall vividly. It needn't be a dramatic, life-changing or epoch-making situation, merely something that you can recall quite easily and in considerable detail – hear the sounds you heard, see the things you saw, feel the things you felt and touch the things you touched at the time of this experience.

Exercise 1.2
Now, for your second writing exercise I want you to write a 'shopping list' of single words or phrases – nothing like a complete sentence – that come to mind as you consider this experience. Make no attempt to 'think' about it consciously or to edit what you write; just record whatever comes to mind and keep the process going for as long as it feels comfortable.

If you were asked to remember the last really good film that you'd seen, the chances of you immediately recalling the beginning of the narrative and then re-playing all the key events in sequence would be pretty rare. I suppose there are some people who do that. But for most of us, what we recall most are key incidents, flash-backs, dramatic sequences and strong visual images.

It's the same with memorable occasions in our lives. We don't recall the past as a linear sequence of events with the mundane and routine interspersed with occasional acts of drama: what we remember is the drama.

Now, what has all this got to do with writing? Well, everything - especially at the 'ideas' stage of writing. What you need to develop is a means of recording your ideas without getting bogged down in all the details. If you want to write a novel, don't start with a piece of paper headed 'Chapter One'. That very rarely works. Instead, keep a notebook, write down odd snatches of dialogue that you imagine or you overhear, make 'shopping list' type notes of incidents you want to write about and most importantly, don't think too closely at this stage of where it's going to go or what it might become. Just make writing – sketching, really – a habit.

What Would a Writer Say?

Ok, so you're jotting down all sorts of things in that nice notebook that you keep especially for the purpose, or else you're scribbling on the backs of envelopes or any other scrap of paper. You're not editing or 'grammatising' anything. You're simply getting the ideas down, shopping-list style. Your life as a writer has begun. The ideas will build, the book will bulge or the pile of paper grow, and the time will come when you know that you're ready to start developing the material you've been gathering.

Great artists do this all the time; they carry sketch books with them and quickly draw a scene or detail that inspires them. Leonardo da Vinci was probably the world's greatest note-book scribbler, and his apparently random jottings, drawings and equations are a record of a mind brimming with ideas. It seemed to come so easily to him. It may not come so easily to the rest of us. So what happens when the notebook pages start to be neglected?

Well, 'write what you know' is the oft-quoted advice. And to the extent that if you're going to write about anything you have to know about it, I suppose that must be true. But you don't – of course – have to know about it *before* you start to think about your writing. Research – the stuff of non-fiction writers of all kinds – is an essential part of the writing process and by 'research' I don't mean sitting in a library for hours or endlessly surfing the internet.

I remember the playwright Jack Rosenthal talking once about why he'd turned down a paid position that would have meant him working office hours. 'I'd miss the school-run,' he explained, 'and that's where I hear some of my best lines…'

The point is we're all living lives that we can use as a source of inspiration or research if we try. Those trees you were looking at earlier, laced with fresh May blossom. What would *a writer* say about them? Now that's notoriously difficult and even the writer Dennis Potter, in his final illness, resorted to describing the apple tree outside his window in Ross-on-Wye as having the 'blossomiest blossom' he had ever seen. But *you're* a writer: what words would *you* use to describe it? And remember, you're not writing in sentences. Not yet.

Exercise 1.3
Have a go at this now. It needn't be blossom, or trees or anything natural. Just pick an object and describe it – shopping-list style – using whatever words occur to you. Keep the object vividly in front of you, either in your imagination, on a photo or looking out of the window. And don't worry if the words seem odd or strange or if you think that no-one else would understand why that word's on your list. Just write.

Of course the time will come when you've got to make those ideas intelligible to other people. And although some of the most satisfying books leave a little bit to the imagination, we don't want to make the reader work too hard. This is where the real craft of writing begins.

Exercise 1.4
Go back to the list you made in response to exercise 1.2. Read the
words again a couple of times. Now try, in your head, to re-create the
narrative (story) of the experience you were recalling. Use your list to
write a paragraph describing in detail what happened. Don't
comment on it or explain anything at this stage (and DON'T EDIT!).
Simply let your mind take you in whichever direction is desires.

Now, depending on your mood/the time of day/your children/the
postman, that exercise can either last for hours or else fizzle out after
a few seconds like a cheap firework. Don't be disheartened. In fact,
be pleased. Either extreme isn't just possible, it's normal – and so is
everything in-between. Make the most of the days when the ideas
flow and things come easily, but be prepared for the days when they
don't. And don't give up – go back. If you can, try doing the last three
exercises in this unit several times; it should yield interesting – and
different – results each time.

Well, that's the end of unit one. I hope you've enjoyed reading; that
you've learnt something and – more than anything – that you keep
writing!

To sum up:

• Don't write!
Writers write, right? Wrong! Humans haven't been writing very long;
our brains aren't adapted to the ways of words on paper (or
computer). To be a successful writer and to capture and preserve your
best ideas, you've got to adapt to the way your brain works: make
lists, doodle, brainstorm. Don't, whatever you do, write ideas down in
full sentences.

• Get the habit.
Don't just stand and gaze at that beautiful sunset, or rage at that
ignorant boy-racer at the traffic lights. Ask yourself: what words
would a *writer* use to write about this experience? Those words may
not come easily at first, but it's a habit – once acquired – that will be
difficult to break.

- And Don't edit.

Not yet, anyway. Editing is as important as (if not more so than) the act of writing, but as the Bible says, there is a time and a place. And this isn't it.

Unit Two: Identify Yourself

In this unit we'll look at how a writer can develop a unique 'voice' and examine the view that what you write about is as important in defining your identity as an author as your style of writing.

Introduction

We're all different. In spite of what I had one of my characters say in 'Writing Therapy', not even identical twins with their exactly-matching DNA turn out to have precisely the same personality. Experiences, however subtly, differ; perspectives change; interpretations vary. It's well-known that witnesses to an accident can often give completely different accounts of what they've seen. And yet they've seen the same thing.

On the face of it then, developing your own 'voice' as an author should be easy. There's no-one quite like you, who thinks the way you do and sees the world through your eyes, interpreting it from your experience. So what you write and the way you write it should be equally unique. But it often isn't, especially at the start of a writing career. And the reasons aren't hard to find.

On The Shelf

If there's one thing wannabee writers are told time and time again, it's 'read read read'. That's good advice: you can't help but learn from reading well-written words in a well-crafted setting and no-one can ever do too much reading. But *what* you read and *why* is the crucial thing to consider when you're writing. How you read is a subject I'll be talking more about in the next session, so for now let's consider the two 'W's'.

Exercise 2.1
What you read...
Take a few moments to consider the kind of things that you like reading. Is there a particular genre or style of writing you enjoy? How catholic are your tastes? And how do you choose the books you read?

Looking at people's bookshelves is a great pastime, and you can tell a lot about a person by the kind of books they read. On my bedside table at the moment, for example, there's a book called 'The English Chorister: A Survey'; Lynn Truss's 'Eats, Shoots and Leaves'; 'Truant' by Horatio Clare, and 'Paperweight' by Stephen Fry. No fiction at the moment, although 'The Kite Runner' is top of the 'to-read' pile. What does that reveal? Well, an interest in the English choral tradition for a start, as well as a tendency to 'catch up' long after the fuss about a book (Kite Runner; Lynn Truss) has died down. It also reveals the kind of books I read because I think I might learn something from them (Horatio Clare) and this little exercise has a dual purpose. You might remember from my initial email that the first week in June (school half-term) is a reading week. Over the next few days I'd like you to consider which single book you'd recommend as being of interest and use to a budding writer. I don't mean 'How To' books as much as those that you think are examples of good practice. Once you've made your choice, introduce yourself to your peer-mentor group and tell them all about it.

If you think we've strayed from the subject of this second session,
think again. Author-voice is probably a function of what we read as
much as who we are, and it's inevitable that we'll try to emulate our
favourite authors, either in style, subject-matter or both. That isn't
necessarily a bad thing. But what IS most certainly a bad thing in any
form of writing is relying on the cliché, and that's what we'll examine
now.

Hot off the Press

Interestingly, the word 'cliché' and its sister 'stereotype' have their
origin in the publishing and writing industry. In the old days of hot
metal printing presses and moveable type, frequently-used phrases
were preserved from one job to the next in order to save them being
set up one letter at a time from scratch. (Oops! *From scratch...* Of
course I mean 'from the beginning' rather than the original sporting
definition of 'to start with no advantage'.)

There's nothing inherently wrong with clichés – the reason they
persist is that they sometimes provide useful shorthand phrases for
common experiences, just as they once provided useful short-cuts for
printers. But they're often over-used to the point where their meaning
changes and becomes unclear, and if there's one thing you don't want
as a writer it's misunderstanding. In addition, don't we owe it to out
readers to be different? If all we're capable of doing is *churning out*
(oops, there I go again!) material that's identical to other people's,
what's the point of writing anything?

Exercise 2.3
For each of these clichéd phrases and expressions, try and write your own unique alternative. Try to be imaginative; think beyond the obvious and be original.

    a) a picture paints a thousand words
    b) as happy as a pig in muck
    c) to start from scratch
    d) out of the frying pan into the fire
    e) don't throw the baby out with the bathwater
    f) never look a gift-horse in the mouth
    g) up and down like a yo-yo

You don't have to re-invent language or re-define the form like a latter-day James Joyce to be different from the rest. Just be yourself. Only *you* see the world your way; make a real effort to find the words that describe what you really mean, and you'll be well on the way to developing your 'author voice'.

It ain't what you say…

Of course it's not just *what* you write, but what you write *about* that defines you as an author. Knowing what to expect from Catherine Cookson, or Margaret Dickinson, has less to do with their style than their subject.

Why is Thomas Hardy considered a great poet, for example? His verse is sometimes twee to the point of being cringe worthy; he contorts syllables and uses outrageous archaisms in the cause of rhythm and rhyme.

> *Thy shadow, earth, from pole to central sea,*
> *Now steals along the moon's meek shine,*
> *In even monochrome and curving line*
> *Of imperturbable serenity.*

So far, so 'Hallmark' greetings card. If that was all there was to Hardy then the big cheeses of twentieth century English poetry (people like Philip Larkin) would hardly have given him a second glance. But then, in verse two things start getting serious:

How shall I link such sun-cast symmetry
With the torn-troubled form I know as thine,
That profile, placid as a brow divine,
With continents of moil and misery?

Now we're into Hardy territory. Faced with a lunar eclipse he not
only wants to record the experience, but examine his own emotional
response and put humanity with all its self-importance in its place.
And then, in the final verse, we get:

Is such the stellar gauge of earthly show?
Nation at war with nation, brains that teem,
Heroes, and women fairer than the skies.

Suddenly we're into new and exciting territory, and those final lines
sum up pretty much entirely Hardy's subject matter, whether as a
novelist or a poet: conflict, brains that teem, heroes... and of course,
women.

And that – more than anything else – is what makes Hardy a great
writer. Not only does he have a consistency of subject-matter over a
lifetime work as a novelist and poet, his subjects are the big ones: life,
death and love.

Exercise 2.4
What kinds of subjects interest you, both as a reader and a writer?
Have you got a particular world view you want to share with your
readers? What – if anything – would you hope someone reading your
work would take from it?

What's it all about?

Lastly, of course, comes the question of why you write, what you
want to write and what you like to read. This is what is sometimes
referred to as an author's 'poetics' and I suppose it's a bit like a brief
literary biography, detailing a writer's author-ly relations and
ambitions as well as their 'theory' of literature in general.

Don't be put off by this, and don't dismiss it either. Taking a moment to think about precisely why you write what you write, what you hope to achieve, why anyone writes and what writing is for is a useful discipline. Many 'writers' (myself included) tend to write first, think afterwards without first having a clear understanding of what it is they're doing. Well, mystery tours can sometimes be quite interesting; but you can also end up hopelessly lost.

Think of this final exercise as your author-manifesto, make it as detailed as you can and share it with your critical partners. That way both you and they will begin to know a little bit about each other, and you will have a clearer idea of where you're going. And knowing your destination is no bad thing at the start of any journey.

Exercise 2.4
Write your own 'poetics' now. What do you think literature is for? Why do you want to be a writer? What experience has brought you to where you are now, and what purpose do you intend your creative work to serve?

Unit Three: Reading as a Writer

This unit builds on the work done in the last session, and develops the idea of reading critically with a writer's eye. What makes a successful book, and can you see 'behind the scenes' and find out how it's done?

Introduction

Reading for writing is not the same as editing. We'll be talking about editing and proof-reading in a later unit. But before ever putting pen to paper, a writer needs to cultivate the same critical faculties as film directors have when watching other people's movies, or car mechanics driving other people's cars or gardeners in other people's gardens. You can admire what you're looking at but you also need to start instinctively asking questions about it, learning from it, and making judgements about it. For an author this means asking questions like:

- *Why* was this book enjoyable?
- *How* does the author keep my interest?
- *What would happen* if one or two words in that paragraph were changed?
- *Why* does the rhythm of a particular sentence flow so smoothly?

Opening Time

Developing this kind of critical eye takes time, but learning to do it can be fun. Here are a few games you can play to get into the mood, so-to-speak…

Exercise 3.1
Choose one of your favourite books; read the opening sentences a couple of times carefully. What (if anything) about the passage makes you want to read on? Is there anything about the words you'd like to change? Could the writing be improved?

Thinking critically about a good book isn't something to feel reticent about. It's an imperfect world, and even the best books contain bad writing; if you're serious about your own writing your antenna should be twitching every time you read something. Admire the greats, by all means, but go beyond mere admiration: why does what you're reading 'work', and what – if anything – could be improved? Thinking like this not only trains your writer's eye, but has the added advantage of making clear that no work of literature is ever faultless, a fact that can be remarkably encouraging to the would-be writer.

Exercise 3.2
Here are a few more opening passages, all taken from well-known novels. If you were browsing in a bookshop, which one would tempt you to read on and why?

i. 'Hole!' said, and then for a change, and with greatly increased emphasis: ''Ole!' He paused, and then broke out with one of his private and peculiar idioms. 'Oh! Beastly Silly Wheeze of a hole.'
ii. He was laughing, chin up, and shaking his head. God the Father was exploding in his face with a glory of sunlight through the painted glass, a glory that moved with his movements to consume and exalt Abraham and Isaac and then God again.
iii. The beginning is simple to mark. We were in sunlight under the turkey oak, partly protected from a strong, gusty wind. I was kneeling on the grass with a corkscrew in my hand, and Clarissa was passing me the bottle – a 1987 Daumas Gassac.
iv. In my younger and more vulnerable years my father gave me some advice that I've been turning over in my mind ever since. 'Whenever you feel like criticising anyone,' he told me, 'just remember that all the people in this world haven't had the advantages that you've had.'

The Meat in the Sandwich

Of course, once you've caught the reader's interest you must work hard to maintain it. The story, the setting, the characterisation, dialogue and explanation all have to pull together in order to ensure the pages keep on being turned. How do the authors you admire do that?

If you're not careful this can begin to turn into literary criticism, which is not the purpose here. Book reviews, magazine articles and academic treatises on an author or a book don't really tell you what a writer needs to know. What you need to do is mentally de-construct the book, search for the joins, see how it's done and learn from what's been written, none of which is easy.

Thankfully, there are a number of things you can do to help make such 'mental undressing' easier. To begin with you can simply pick up a book you admire and go looking for clues. What makes the experience of reading enjoyable? Why is the story so satisfying? What is it about the author's style that you enjoy?

If an entire book seems daunting, take a sample passage and examine it in detail. And examine it with a purpose. One way to do this is to re-write the passage, making deliberate changes 'for better or worse' (as the prayer book says about a different subject).

Exercise 3.4

Take a favourite passage from a book: any book, any genre, published or unpublished, your own, someone else's, finished or a work-in-progress. First, go through the passage asking yourself the kind of questions listed above. If it's a piece of your own work, be as ruthless and dispassionate as possible.

Next, the fun part. Re-write the passage a couple of times, making deliberate changes. You could insert adverbs, change the sex or name of the protagonist(s), change the setting, alter the tense, change the perspective (e.g. first to third person) - anything. Enjoy this, and be as outrageous as you can!

Here's an extract from my novel, Writing Therapy*, as an example. First, the original:

> *'Who's your captain?' somebody was saying.*
> *'I am,' Ted replied.*
> *'Ok, then – heads or tails?'*
> *Ted lost. We fielded first. Or rather, most of us just stood around and waited for the ball to come in our direction. Fielding implies a certain dynamism which was sadly lacking in our team's efforts. Lizzie, for a start, kept running in the wrong direction. Now, there are studies suggesting anorexics have a problem with basic navigation. Back then it was just another source of irritation.*
> *'Lizzie – watch the ball!' Ted shouted as she missed another catch.*
> *The rehab team were good. They enjoyed Ted's bowling, hitting him so far that sometimes they were able to complete a double rounder, or whatever.*
> *'Thirty-nine to win then,' Mrs Lotinga was trilling as we lined up to take our turn at batting.*
> *Ted went first, and scored a couple before holing out to someone in the deep. The rehab team could catch. I went in next. I thought I did ok. I scored a few more – so did everybody, even Lizzie. But gradually we began to fall away, either run-out, caught or – in the case of Debbie - missing the ball completely.*

Jane was last in. Three more needed, and some tricky bowling still to come. She set herself, then whacked the ball and started running. Ted was screaming, but Jane wasn't awfully athletic. A fielder in the deep was returning the ball just as she set off from the penultimate base. With a flourish the fielder at fourth base collected the ball and demolished the post.

'Oh bad luck Jane,' Sophie shouted. 'Yeah, well tried!' we echoed.

All that is, except for Ted. He stormed off the field, marching straight back to the adolescent unit, missing the post-match party.

'I remember that,' said Sophie.

'It was quite amusing, really. And, do you remember how - once he'd gone - we started talking about him?'

'Someone said how childish his behaviour was.'

'Yes, we all joined in, including Jane.'

'All,' I said, 'except for Monica.'

Monica had been listening.

Now, here's the same passage with some changes:

When we arrived, somebody asked who our team's captain was. Ted, of course, immediately said it was him before anyone else had a chance to speak, just like he lost the toss and announced that he would be our bowler.

That meant we all had to stand around and wait for the ball to come in our direction, which was something else that annoyed Ted. You couldn't really call it fielding. 'Fielding' implies a certain dynamism which was sadly lacking in our team's efforts. Lizzie, for example, just kept running in the wrong direction. There have been studies suggesting anorexics have a problem with basic navigation. Back then it was just another source of irritation and Ted kept shouting at her as she ran the wrong way for a catch.

The rehab team were good. They enjoyed Ted's bowling, hitting him so far that sometimes they were able to complete a double rounder, or whatever it's called. By the end of their innings they'd scored thirty-eight, which gave us a target of thirty-nine.

Ted batted first, and scored a couple before holing out to someone in the deep. The rehab team could catch. I went in next. I thought I did ok. I scored a few more – so did everybody, even Lizzie. But gradually we began to fall away, either run-out, caught or – in the case of Debbie - missing the ball completely.

Jane was last in. Three more needed, and some tricky bowling still to come. She set herself, then whacked the ball and started running. Ted was screaming, but Jane wasn't awfully athletic. A fielder in the deep was returning the ball just as she set off from the penultimate post. With a flourish the fielder at fourth base collected the ball and demolished the post.

'Oh bad luck Jane,' Sophie shouted. 'Yeah, well tried!' we echoed.

All that is, except for Ted. He stormed off the field, marching straight back to the adolescent unit, missing the post-match party. It was quite amusing, really. Once he'd gone we started talking about him. Someone said how childish his behaviour was. We all joined in, including Jane.

All, that is, except for Monica.

Before anyone gets the wrong idea I should point out that I've chosen a passage from one of my books for two simple reasons: one, I own the copyright and can quote extensively, and two, I already have a ready-made 're-write' of that passage, so I'm cheating! Which version works 'best' depends on a number of different factors, but the first – with dialogue, 'showing' rather than telling – would generally be regarded as superior. Personally, I quite like the alternative, narrative passage and I'm glad I didn't delete it. But it shows how different the same thing can be, and this is an exercise you should try and repeat several times with different passages, changing different things each time.

To sum up…

- Reading for writing starts when you begin to ask questions like 'why does this passage work?' and 'what would happen if it was changed?'
- You can practise reading for writing in a number of ways, including 're-writing' passages of well-known works.
- Even the 'best' writers' work can sometimes be improved.

Unit Four: Fact and Fiction

- *Where does fact end and fiction begin?*
- *How are the two genres related and can you be good at writing both?*
- *What makes good writing 'true'?*

Introduction

'There's no such thing as fiction, only fact gone wrong....'

An extreme view perhaps, but the dividing line between fact and fiction is never clear, and fiction-writers are notorious for raiding their own (and other people's) lives for the sake of a good story. This session, I suppose, is as much about inspiration as different types of writing, which is appropriate when you consider the fact that the differences between the two are often only superficial.

Many great works of fiction have been thinly disguised fact, and many a so-called true story has been embellished to the point of becoming more fantasy than reality. Consider George Orwell's classic Animal Farm. On the face of it, it's a book about farmyard animals taking over a farm, but of course it goes much deeper than that and is in fact a thinly-disguised account of the Russian revolution. One of the first 'novels' (if not *the* first) ever written – Robinson Crusoe – was thought to have been based on the real life experience of one Henry Pitman, sometime surgeon and Monmouth rebel. To illustrate the close connections between fact and fiction, try this short exercise in both.

Exercise 4.1
Think of a real character from your own life: a relative or friend, but someone with a strong personality about whom plenty can be written. Now write a mini biography (the kind of thing you see in concert programmes, or on the back of books). Next consider what you would have to do to fictionalise it – change the names, perhaps, and other telling details while retaining the arc of the biography. Then write it out a second time as if it were a work of fiction.

Tell all the truth, but tell it slant...

Because there never was (and probably never will be) a farm in which the animals turned on their human masters, can *Animal Farm* be true? If a story hasn't happened in reality, is it a lie? Without getting too philosophical, we need to consider briefly the relationship between truth and fiction and establish a couple of basic rules. Any parent reading fairy tales to their children (or even watching certain children's' television programmes) can't fail to be aware of the 'messages' such stories contain. It doesn't really matter if there really was a boy who cried wolf; the truth of the tale is universal. Good literature is just like this: it tells us something about human nature that is true irrespective of the factual details of the story. King Lear (indeed, most of Shakespeare) might say more about the workings of the human mind than an entire library of psychological case-notes. There are vanities, jealousies, struggles, triumphs and disasters that pass through the generations like the words in a stick of seaside rock. Good fiction holds a mirror to these truths, and thus is 'true' but in a different way to factual writing.

Non-fiction – to the extent that it is worth reading – seeks to do a similar kind of thing. Whether it is history, biography, autobiography or literary analysis, good non-fiction writing involves teasing out the universal truths of the human condition and showing them in a particular setting.

Exercise 4.2
Think of an incident from your own life – or the life of someone close to you – that was typical in some way of the experience of almost everyone. Maybe a first experience of love and loss; a time when pride came before a fall; a solemn warning that went unheeded (but proved to be accurate); a sacrifice made for the good of someone else. Write this incident up as if it had happened to someone else, either a well-known character from fiction (books or television) or somebody known to you. Try writing it in the third person ('She knew when she woke up that something was wrong') as a way of further distancing yourself from the experience, but don't worry if this proves difficult. Be aware of what the moral of the story is supposed to be, and remain true to that.

The Devil is in the Detail

Without straying far from the theme of this week's lesson, it'd be worth considering for a moment what it takes to make a character in a piece of writing – any writing: fact or fiction – seem 'real' to the reader. If you were a historian and you wanted to capture the essence of a great historical figure, or a biographer keen to bring alive the subject of your biography or a novelist desperate to make your characters come alive, what is it that you have to do?

The answer is surprisingly similar in all three cases. There's no 'magic wand' to be waved which makes a character – fictional or real – come alive on the page, but there are one or two tricks to be learnt which can help pull the rabbit from the hat.

Exercise 4.3
If you're working on a piece of fiction, choose a character from a story that you've written or that you are writing. If you're not writing fiction, choose a character from whatever form you're working in. Now construct a CV for that person: include everything that an employer would expect to see – the person's education, where they went to school, what qualifications they gained; work experience – the jobs they've done, for how long and so on; their interests and achievements – county colours for athletics, a passion for pressing wild flowers; and finally, a personal statement – what would this character say about themselves if they were applying for a job. Make the job up if you find that helps.

This is the kind of thing writers do all the time. Of course, if you're dealing with a real person the 'facts' will already be available. But presenting them in such a format can reveal a few surprises. For a fictional character, such details might not ever feature in the narrative you're creating. But knowing them means that your writing will be more convincing.

Taking Shape

In fiction, of course, things happen in a particular way for the sake of a satisfying story. Real-life seldom presents us with a logical narrative sequence which can be transferred directly to the page. The art of great story-telling (whether in a novel or a work of history or biography) is keeping the reader or listeners' interest, which means giving shape and structure to a story.

Little has changed in this regard for thousands of years. The early Greek epics, the Norse Sagas, early Romances and the first novels all tend to follow a very simple three act narrative structure:

1. Set up
2. Confrontation
3. Resolution

Exercise 4.4
Go back through a couple of books you've recently finished and see if you can make them fit this three-act structure. Is it easy or difficult, and what does that say about the quality of the book you've chosen?

Of course there are a thousand different ways of doing this, which is why there are so many good books. We'll examine plot and structure in more detail in a later unit, but for now it is enough to appreciate that – whatever form of writing you're engaged in – you need to tell a story, fact or fiction, in a structured way.

Exercise 4.5
Decide now what you'd like to spend your 'free' week doing. Of course, being half-term this might not be a decision entirely under your control, but however busy you might be, try to ring-fence a small amount of time to pursue one of the options – either reading (as a writer) or writing.

To sum up...

- The dividing-line between fact and fiction is often thinner than we realise, and most writers plunder real-life for their stories;

- Just because something hasn't happened, doesn't mean it isn't true. One of the great purposes of fiction is to reveal universal truths about the human condition, a purpose often achieved more easily through a cast of fictional characters;

- Character creation – whether real or imagined – is the central task of any prose writer and can be helped by considering a wide range of details, many of which will never figure in the finished manuscript;

- All stories have a structure: real-life must be edited to fit, and fiction must present the reader with a satisfying narrative to keep the pages turning.

Unit Five: Reading Week

Unit Six: Verse and Worse

- *Does a poem have to rhyme?*
- *How do you detect the rhythm in a poem?*
- *What makes a poem different from prose and what use is poetry to the committed prose-writer?*

Introduction

Of all the units in this brief course, this is probably the most specialist. Poetry can be a bit of a Marmite area, and even people who like it, write it and are otherwise 'into' it often have strong views and can be very defensive about them. Take the first question (above)? Does a poem have to rhyme? For some people, that's everything: no rhyme = no poem. But Shakespeare didn't rhyme; not all the time. So what actually makes poetry different from prose?

The Rhythm of Life

What's the difference between the following sentences?

- The boy stood on the burning deck
- The boy was standing on the burning deck
- The deck around the boy was burning

Ok, too easy. But useful, I hope. Of course, all three sentences have rhythm: all sentences do, to some degree. But the first (the one that everyone knows) has a regular beat and a forward momentum which is usually the mark of good poetry. (I'm not saying, necessarily, that *Casabianca* is a great poem, or that Felicia Dorothea Hemans was a great poet although – incidentally – her 'Landing of the Pilgrim Fathers in New England' has assumed the status almost of a sacred text in the USA, despite her never having been there.)

Let's look at that first line again:
The **BOY** stood **ON** the **BURN**ing **DECK**

There is a fairly clear four-stress rhythm in that line; the next line

Whence **ALL** but **HE** had **FLED**

…has only three stresses, and you'll notice that each 'dum' (what we poets *ahem* call a 'foot') is preceded by an unstressed syllable (a 'de').

This is called ballad metre (or Common Metre, abbreviated C.M. in things like hymn books) and is the 'de-dum, de-dum, de-dum, de-dum' pattern that almost everybody recognises.

Technically, we could say that the first line of *Casiabanca* is an iambic tetrameter and the second, an iambic trimeter and that the rhyming pattern is abab, but we won't. I think we'll leave that to the advanced course. If there is one.

The point is that there is a deliberate – and memorable – rhythm to the line which is part of its appeal. Arranging words in order – whether as a poet or a prose writer – is more than a matter of merely transmitting information. Rearranging or changing words (as I did, above) can subtly alter the rhythm of a sentence and make it more or less effective.

Rhyme Time

Actually, that sub-heading is rather misleading. The subject of rhyme and its many variations would take an entire course to cover. Suffice to say that words rhyme in a variety of ways (some of which aren't considered 'proper' by poetry purists) but the simple reason for getting words to rhyme is this: so you can remember them. Rhyming dates from a time when all literature was transmitted orally and was done to make large tracts of 'writing' easier to remember. It's been used as a teaching tool for thousands of years, which is why many religious tracts seem to have echoes (if not overt traces) of the poetry they once were.

Of course, the fact that we can now commit words to paper and have little need for rote learning isn't the only reason rhyme has come to be seen as less than essential in poetry, but it is undoubtedly a factor. As we've seen, the rhythm of a sentence is a vitally important element in poetry, and can easily supplant the need for rhyme. But together, they're a powerful combination and worthy of examination.

Exercise 6.2
Try rhyming the following words: car; tree; red; box; ice; flower;
moaning; windmill; railway; service.

Even a simple task like that should reveal one important detail about rhyme: single syllables are (generally) easier than multiples, and if you can only rhyme the last syllable of any of the polysyllabic words, you're guilty of a half-rhyme. But does any of that matter?

Are you Free?

Poetry, verse, call it what you will, now comes in lots of different shapes and sizes. The rhythm of the words is vital, but the rhyme can sometimes be dispensed with. When it is, it's often referred to as 'free verse' for the simple reason that it's free of rhyme.

It's at this point that we're as near as we're going to get to answering the last of this session's three questions: what's the difference between poetry and prose, and is the latter any use to prose writers? And to answer it, I'm going to quote a short passage from a book by Roger Deakin, *Waterlog*:

> *The restless Dorset sea fondles and gropes*
> *at the rock-shelf like a lover's hand*
> *up a stockinged thigh...*
>
> *The snowy waves shampoo over the rocks*
> *And waterfall off its seaward rim.*

I wonder what you decided and why, and if you'd be surprised to learn that – whatever your choice, you're probably right. Rather unfairly, I arranged the lines on the page to look like poetry, but they're actually from a work entirely written in prose. But - revealingly – the late Roger Deakin once revealed in an interview that his writing notes were quite often written in the form of poetry. Not, perhaps, the 'de-dum, de-dum, de-dum' poetry of Casiabanca, still less the kind of poetry that rhymes (obviously) but poetry, nevertheless: the words pass themselves off quite convincingly as verse not just because they may first have been written that way, but because of the intense, poetic focus of the imagery and the almost luxuriant use of simile. It's far more concentrated than you'd normally get in prose, and an entire book written like that would be a tad indigestible. But as a way of sketching – quickly – a situation and recording as much information as possible, poetry is a handy addition to any prose-writer's tool-kit.

Poetry is extremely personal, and if you aren't sure you want to share it with any of your group I'm sure no-one will mind. But if you do, let it go: see if other people 'get' it, and if they do, then you're launched on a career in poetry.

Summary

- Poems don't have to rhyme, but all poems must have a recognisable rhythm;
- The stronger the rhythm (of whatever pattern) the better, generally, the poem;
- In some ways, poetry is like prose, distilled. Its focus can be a useful tool for any writer.

Unit Seven: How very Novel

This week we take a closer look at fiction, examining different styles and genres and the question of sustained writing.

- *What is a 'novel' and how long has the form been around?*
- *What are the different types of fiction and how strong are the boundaries?*
- *How is a novel constructed?*
- *How do I start writing a novel, and what's the secret of sustained writing?*

Introduction

In the grand scheme of things, the sustained prose fiction work – or 'novel' as we know it – hasn't been around for very long. Until approximately 250 years ago if you wanted fiction, you either went to the theatre or listened to a bard recite one of the epics (if you were of a Lordly disposition) or else sing a ballad. And there was one very good reason for that: most people couldn't read and if they could, they'd be reading things like the Bible. There wasn't much else available.

The first novel in English is generally thought to be *Robinson Crusoe*, by Daniel Defoe. Of course, that depends how you define a 'novel' and as that's the subject of this week's session, it's an apposite place to start thinking.

Exercise 7.1
What is a novel? What makes a novel different from other works of literature, and how do you know when you're reading a novel? Try making a list of some of the common characteristics of the novels you read, and then see if you can find an example that doesn't tick all the boxes.

Does it have to be in prose? Does it have to be entirely fictional? How long does a novel have to be? These aren't easy questions, but most critics generally think that a novel should be almost entirely prose and almost entirely fictional. This excludes the re-telling of an epic like *La Morte d'Arthur* (1485) or Chaucer, which would otherwise knock *Crusoe* off his perch. And let's not forget that we're talking here about the English novel: Boccaccio's Decameron (which seems to have influenced Chaucer) dates from 1353.

As for length, a novel is usually more than 50,000 words long and can be anything up to 150,000 words or more. The 'average' (such as it is) varies for different genres of fiction, but is usually thought to be around 80,000 words.

Genres

Humans seem to like things to be stored away in neat categories. Ever since Adam was given the job of naming all the animals in *Genesis*, we've been making lists and inventing classifications. Books are no different. There are horror stories, romances, erotic fiction, chick lit, the historical novel, science fiction, lad lit and literary fiction to name just a few. And you don't have to analyse your own reading habits to see where your preference lies: just look at the back cover of the books you're reading and you'll find a helpful little label designed to help the book-shop or the library put it on the right shelf.

Is any of this important? Well, yes. Some genres have their own conventions and while it's perfectly acceptable to push the boundaries, if you're writing a thriller and you don't at least know the kind of short-hand references or genre clichés that are popular, you're at a disadvantage. So it's worth thinking about the type of book you're writing, not because you want it to be like all the other books in that particular genre, but so that you have a clear idea what readers of books like yours want to read. And if you're not sure what kind of book you're writing, call it 'literary' fiction. No-one's ever going to contradict you!

Nuts and Bolts

Although they're all different (or should be: they're not called 'novels' for nothing!) most books share certain common features which are regarded pretty much as essential for their success. This doesn't mean that all successful books are built the same way, as anyone who's ever tried reading *Ulysses* will know. But the following elements are useful to consider even if you plan a grand literary gesture.

Structure

Read ten different novels and – if you're choosing carefully – you could find ten different types of structure. Which isn't very helpful if you're learning the craft. Writers and tutors often refer to the 'arc' of the story, which in its simplest form is:

1. Set up
2. Confrontation
3. Resolution

Basically, if you're writing a novel (as opposed to, say, a short story) you've got to take the reader on a bit of a holiday: short-stories are away-days; novels are the full vacation and *War and Peace* is the year-long world cruise. Which means there's got to be plenty going on: there will be sub-plots, apparent solutions (which turn out to be anything but) and real emotional development.

And don't forget the three act structure doesn't have to happen in that order: some books (and quite a few films) start the action at the final destination and then reveal how the characters arrived there. Or you could open with a confrontation and follow with the set up, or background information. Whatever you do, remember your story can't just 'happen'. You have to craft it into a satisfying piece of entertainment, which will mean teasing the reader a little. No-one pays to see a strip-tease if it doesn't: an author needs to know what to reveal and when, and only get his kit off in the final chapter!

Perspective

First-person, second-person, third-person? For most novels it's either the former or the latter. Sometimes it's a combination of the two. Rarely, but interestingly, a novel will be written in the second-person – 'You hated Spain; you said it would be fine but for the Spaniards'. Your choice of perspective depends on the kind of story you're trying to tell. If you really want to get in the central character's skin, first-person might be the way to go. You can decide if you want the narrator to be reliable or not according to the story that you're telling. For example, if you're writing about childhood infatuation it, telling the story directly via an obviously delusional narrator will be an effective strategy. On the other hand, a third-person narrator might be able to tell the reader things about the central character which even they don't know. This kind of all-knowing (or 'omniscient') narration is probably most common.

Description

Without turning on the purple prose, every author needs to think carefully about descriptive passages. On a blog post a while ago I played a game of 'choose ten books a writer ought to read'; one was a Windsor and Newton watercolour pad. I was only half-joking. To describe anything, you've got to look and look again. Don't glance, then glance away and begin writing. Doing that will almost certainly lead to the kind of clichéd descriptions any author might have penned. Of course, certain similes and metaphors seem to lend themselves to descriptive prose: as smooth as silk; as happy as a sand-boy; like a mill-pond. But what marks a really creative writer is choosing some new and exciting comparison: something that makes the reader sit up and think 'yes – I'd never noticed that before or thought about it in that way, but that's true!' Try to make descriptive prose informative and original.

Characterisation

Perhaps the most important element in the novel is the presentation and development of the protagonists – characterisation. Bringing a character to life and presenting them as someone engaging and memorable to the reader is the real magic of the novel. It brings together the previous three elements and quite simply makes or breaks a novel. I remember an early editor's report on my own novel in which a reader had said of my narrator: 'on page 102 she tries to kill herself and – to be blunt – I wish that she'd succeeded.' Oh dear!

Of course you can't please all the people all the time. One reason I don't read much romantic fiction is that I find it hard to identify – still less sympathise – with the characters. But whether they're good or bad, float everybody's boat or leave them wanting less, your characters must be strong. There's really only one trick to make characters strong: know everything about them. Everything: what colour pants they're wearing, whether they prefer dogs to cats, like Marmite, eat with their fingers while watching the telly and have a secret obsession with Australian cricketers. And let's be clear about this: just because you know it doesn't mean it's going in the book. But because you know it, what does go in the book will be a darn sight more convincing.

Carry On... Writing

Ok, so you've started. Believe it or not, that's the easy bit. Now you've got to carry on. Sustaining a work of fiction for 50, 60, 70 or 80 thousand words is a feat of endurance and if you're finding it hard to keep going there could be a number of reasons. Are you finding it interesting? If not, give up; neither will your readers. Are you blocked? If so, just write; write gobble-di-gook; write rubbish; just write *something*. Most writers find starting again after a break a little difficult. Many suggest leaving the story at a point at which you know what's going to happen next; that way, you'll have an easy start next time. I've even heard of writers who stop mid-sentence. Little tricks like that can make it easier to pick up the next day.

You'll notice there's a distinct lack of writing exercises this week. There are two reasons for that. One, I hope you're actively working on something that you intend to submit for publication. We'll talk in more detail about that in a couple of weeks. Second, you can make an exercise out of any one of the sections of this week's course, and I'd rather you did. I hope something has struck a chord in relation to your own work. Rather than be led by things marked 'exercise' I hope you'll be able to take some of the material as the starting point for doing something we'll be looking at more closely next week: editing your work.

To sum up...

- The novel as an art-form is relatively new and is evolving all the time; there are boundaries and common elements and themes, but be prepared to break the mould;
- If you are planning something new, know which mould you're breaking. Genres are convenient pigeon-holes but they exist for a reason. At the very least, they can tell you what a group of readers enjoy reading;
- Of all the bits that go to make up a good novel, characterisation is the most important. Just as you might expect to know your best friend or partner intimately, make sure you know everything about your central character;
- Writing a novel is like running a marathon: you're going to hit a wall somewhere; write through it, and there are a number of tricks you can use to help you.

Unit Eight: Be your own editor

Any form of writing should be the best that you can make it before considering submitting to editors, publishers etc. Learn how to examine your own work critically and dispassionately.

Introduction

What is an editor, and what do they do? No doubt a great many authors have a positive relationship with a tactful but perceptive editor who sees it as his or her job to gently act as midwife at the birth of a new literary masterpiece. But there are some who seem to think their job is more important than the author's. If you're lucky and you land someone in the former category, you're home and dry; if not, and your work crosses the desk of someone struggling with too many authors in too many different genres, you'll be thankful that you spent time editing, re-editing and editing again yourself before you submitted. And that's not easy.

But it is essential.

Exercise 8.1
Imagine the Rev. W. Awdry has just delivered the latest 'Thomas' epic to your office. What do you do with the following lines?

> *'Thomas loved taking the children in his carriages. He rushed off as quickly as he could to the station. He arrived at the station in no time. The children were all waiting for him. They cheered when they saw him arrive.'*

Of course, there's nothing wrong with what the Rev. Awdry has written. But wouldn't this be a little more, well… interesting?

'Thomas loved taking the children in his carriages, so he hurried as quickly as he could to the station. He arrived in no time and the children cheered as soon as they saw him arrive.'

Simple, but effective – and that's what an editor's there to do: iron out the creases; ensure the story flows; ensure that there's consistency between each section of the book (e.g. the central character doesn't suddenly lose three years in age between chapters one and ten). And you can do it for yourself! Maybe not as well as a professional editor, but well enough to make your eventual experience with one more rewarding for both of you.

Step away from the computer

The first thing you need to do – it's not an option – is forget about it, put the book away, hide the poem in a drawer, bury that story or article under a pile of laundry. And do something else. Anything: writing, reading, rock-climbing if you so choose. But don't even think about getting out that magnum opus. Leave it. Let it grow. Your first draft is a bit like a seed, and committing it to paper is like planting it in fertile soil. You water it, of course; but then you leave it. You don't pull it up at the first sign of green shoots to see how it's doing.

Exercise 8.2
Of course, in the heat of the creative moment it can be difficult to leave a piece of creative writing, especially when you know that it needs more work. Perhaps you've got a long-neglected piece of writing mouldering in a drawer somewhere or hidden in a long-forgotten folder on your computer? Dig it out now, and read it afresh; what changes would you make as your own editor? It should be a lot easier to see what needs doing after distancing yourself from what you've written.

Of course, that's not all a good editor will do. As a dispassionate reader (as well as an experienced one) a good editor will be able to see your book through the eyes of the market: they'll understand what works and what doesn't, and will be able to advise accordingly. This isn't something many writers can achieve by themselves.

But who said anything about doing it by yourself? You'll have friends and acquaintances you can call on: call on them. Choose carefully; you don't want a negative opinion to spoil a good relationship. But you should be able to think of someone not too close (but close enough) to read what you've written and give you an honest opinion. If they're willing, make it clear what you want from them. You need someone to give it to you straight: does it work? are there any problems? what improvements can you make?

*Think about this now. Who could you call on to give you an honest –
and accurate – opinion of your work? Cast the net far and wide and
be prepared to consider people who might not otherwise be among
your intimate circle – they could be the most useful!*

The Devil is in the Detail

Style is subjective, and what one reader – or editor – admires can be
anathema to another. There's no accounting for taste. What you can
do, however, is make your prose as accurate as possible. There are
several good books on the market without resorting to Lynne Truss's
rather pedantic 'Eats, Shoots and Leaves'. The truth is, the English
language is dynamic, evolving all the time in the light of trends (like
text-speak) and the influence of other languages. (Our vocabulary is
generally thought to be at least half a million words strong, compared
to, say, French with only a tenth of that.) Shakespeare alone was
responsible for at least 2000 neologisms (new words) many of which
were, undoubtedly, dialect words which he brought to a wider
audience.

So, we oughtn't to be too precious about the language. But there are
certain basic standards a writer ought to strive to meet. And here are a
few of the most common mistakes to keep as a check-list. If you can't
be your own editor, at least be your own sub:

> *Accommodate*
> *Achievable*
> *Acquired*
> *Aggravate*
> *Appropriately*
>
> *Benefited*
> *Biased or biassed (both are correct)*
> *Bored with (not of)*
> *Bare all/one's soul (not bear)*
> *Business*
>
> *Commendable*
> *Committed*
> *Conscientious*

Creditable

Debatable
Definite
Desperate
Diligence
Diligent

Eliminate
Equalise (Equalize in the US)
Exaggerate

Focused, focussed (either is acceptable)

Forty
Four
Fulfil
Fulfilled
Fulfilling
Fulfilment

Hear, hear (not here, here)
Humorous
Humour

Immediately
Independent
Industriously
Ineligible
Intelligent
Intelligible

(un)necessarily
(un)necessary

Occasional
Occasionally
Occur
Occurred

Occurrence
Occurring

Perceive

Perception
Perceptive

Practice (noun) 'He needs practice; with practice she will...'
Practise (verb) 'He needs to practise; she must practise...'

Resourceful

Separate

Thorough

And beware the spell-check. How many disciples did Jesus have? None, but he had twelve fully-committed decibels.

And as for the apostrophe...

We all do it. I did it earlier in this course, and it cost me a couple of copies of 'Writing Therapy'. That darned comma in the air can be a real menace; most of us know (even if we make mistakes when typing quickly) the difference between you're (you are) and your (as in, belonging to you). It's (it is) the possessive apostrophe that really creates problems. And if it does for you, it might help to know that it's (it is... that's – that is - an exception to the rule!) is a relic of an archaic way of speaking. Several hundred years ago, the possessive was rendered (largely) with an extra 'e'. So, the swill of the pigs would be 'pigges swill' and the apostrophe (') simply became a shorthand to replace the 'e'. Thus the 'groceres apostrophe' is now the 'grocer's apostrophe' and the (') replaces the missing letter just as it does when you say 'it's – it is – a fine day'.

To sum up...

- Take the greatest care with what you do, and check it when you can. Put it away, and get others whose opinion you can trust, to read what you've written before showing it to anyone in the industry;
- Avoid the common pitfalls. A simple grammar (-ar, not –er!) can help, but – as ever – practice (-ice, ice baby!) makes perfect.
- The English language isn't precious; we don't have an *Academy Anglaise* to protect it (like the French) but it pays to stick to certain rules. In particular, you aren't ever 'bored of' something (like this writing course) – you are bored with it.

Unit Nine: Towards publication

A look at the world of publishing in general as well as an invitation to consider a piece of your own work for publication in the course anthology.

Introduction

Publication is the Holy Grail for many writers. They might tell you it's their 'passion for words' and the 'need to write' that keeps them going. But what they really want is publication, which is entirely understandable. After all, what's the point of writing if nobody's reading? (Well, of course, there *is* a point and there are writers happy to do it for its own sake, but that's another story.) But what does 'being published' actually mean? If you're a blogger, every time you write a post you hit the 'publish' button and your words are flung into cyberspace for all to see. And anyone can publish themselves these days on Lulu, a service we'll examine in a bit more detail later. Getting published isn't only difficult to achieve, it's difficult to define.

Dear Sir or Madam

I suppose anything that gets your work 'out there' where it can be seen, discussed, enjoyed and – perhaps – paid for counts as being published. Traditionally, though, publication has meant – for books – someone else (the publisher) taking up your work and taking a financial risk by having it type-set, printed, bound and distributed. You, the author, then receive a fraction of the cover price of each book sold in royalties. So it's in your interests both to choose a publisher capable of the widest distribution and to get involved with the promotion of your own book. If only it was all that simple.

In reality, if you're writing fiction, you'll have to have completed your novel, edited it to within an inch of its life and ironed out every single typo, erased each grammatical infelicity, and written a synopsis before you even think about approaching someone with a view to publication. For non-fiction, things are a little different and – in general – you'll be expected to provide a detailed, chapter-by-chapter outline of the book together with a market analysis (who's going to buy it when it's finished?) and at least one sample chapter. On the basis of this outline, a publisher may invite you – with or without obligation – to submit the whole thing at a later date (i.e. when it's written). Magazines and periodicals often work in a similar way: an editor will want to hear your ideas first (and be persuaded not only that the article is worth writing, but that you're the person to write it).

All this can be quite daunting, and the odds against getting a new work of fiction by an unknown author even read by a major publisher are tiny. Be prepared to wallpaper your sitting room with your rejection letters – if you get any! Some publishers are too 'busy' even for that courtesy. And be prepared to wait… and wait… and wait. It can take an inordinate amount of time even to get a response. No wonder some authors get impatient.

Exercise 9.2
Publishing is changing. Technological advances mean books can be economically produced in units as small as a single copy! There can be a lot to take in, but it's worth knowing a little about the industry you hope to be involved in. How much, for instance, do you know about each of the following?
> *Print-runs*
> *Slush pile*
> *Distribution*
> *Type-setting*
> *Print-on-demand*
> *Proof-reading*
> *ISBN*
> *Vanity publishing*
> *Copyright*

Go Your Own Way

Just as blogging democratises on-line publishing, technology now means that if you're fed up waiting, you could – if you go into it with your eyes wide open – guarantee seeing your book in print, and a lot quicker than if you approach a traditional publisher. Lulu.com is perhaps the best-known self-publishing service, with Amazon's Createspace doing something similar. Print-on-demand technology (as used by Lulu) means that a publisher no longer has to take a financial risk printing lots of books that people might not buy. If someone wants your book, it's printed; it's as simple as that.

Of course, it's also more expensive doing it that way (which is one reason traditional publishers don't do it) and the shipping costs from Lulu.com – which still seems to have no UK POD-partner – can be extortionate. And it also means that – as author – the hard work of writing a book doesn't end with the last full-stop. You'll be responsible for cover-design, typesetting (simple enough using Lulu's software) and – and herein lies the rub – sales.

Exercise 9.3
If you haven't already done so, have a look at Lulu.com now. Sign up for an account – it's free – and have a play with their software. It can be revealing to see how your book might look even if you intend to go down the traditional publishing route when it's finished, and it'll begin to give you some insight into what is – for most authors – post-production of their work.

Money, Money, Money

Some books sell themselves; if you're well-known for misbehaving in West End night-clubs or parading in front of several million voyeurs on programmes like 'Big Brother' then you'll find the media beating a path to your door once they know you've got a book out. (Whether you've written the book yourself or whether it's any good won't matter!) But for the rest of us, selling our wares is essential – and this goes for everyone, however published. Even if Harper Collins makes you an offer you can't refuse, they'll expect you to be heavily involved with the publicity and promotion activities they've got planned. But then, at least they've planned them. If you're doing it alone, you've got to be your own publicist as well, and we'll discuss some of the dark arts of self-promotion in the final session.

Whatever happens, don't assume that once your book hits the shelves you'll be instantly handing in your resignation from the day job. Authors in the UK earn an average of £16,531 according to a recent survey. But the top 10% of them earn more than 50% of total income made from writing, while the bottom 50% earn less than 10% of it. And - at least in some cases - for 'author' read 'celebrity employing a ghost-writer'. Cynical? Me? Possibly.

You're So Vain

I bet you think this course is about you? Don't you? Seriously though, while we're on the subject of publishing, self-publishing, Lulu, money and the like can I make one thing clear? If someone asks you to pay – 'contribute towards' – the costs of publication don't go anywhere near it. Ok, so if you want an ISBN and certain distribution packages with Lulu, for example, then you'll have to pay for them. But paying for an ISBN isn't the same as paying for the editing, printing, marketing, distributing and storing of your book and there are plenty of outfits out there who'll send you flattering letters before asking you to stump up at least a grand for a modest print-run of 500 books. Don't. If you're desperate to see yourself in print, go to Lulu or Amazon, where you pay your own costs, and take your own profits. In the world of books and publishing there are seldom areas of complete agreement on anything – except vanity publishing. It's always a bad idea, in spite of the fact that – historically – several well-known authors did it. They had to. They didn't have Lulu.

The Final Curtain?

Neither did they have Dotterel Press, of course, and an anthology toshow-off their talents. Thank you to everyone who has already submitted something for consideration. This is now starting to take shape as a really exciting show-case for some seriously good writing. So, if you want to get published in time for Christmas, take a look at the Dotterel Press blog (http://dotterelpress.blogspot.com/) and website (http://www.dotterelpress.com/) for further details. We're accepting everything – short stories, poems, memoirs – and would love to see what you've got to offer. Just remember what was said last week – make everything you submit the best that it can be before you hit 'send'. And we'll do the rest. And instead of summing up this week, here are a few websites you might like to explore:

YouWriteOn http://www.youwriteon.com/
Authonomy http://www.authonomy.com/
CompletelyNovel http://www.completelynovel.com/
The Literary Consultancy http://www.literaryconsultancy.co.uk/
WriteThisMoment http://www.writethismoment.com/

Keep writing!

Unit Ten: I Did It My Way

The end – or the beginning? Keeping the writing habit and the learning process going.

Introduction

I can't quite believe the adventure that has been the creative writing e-course is almost over. Three months after rather hastily responding to a disappointed tweet by @caroljs (whose creative writing evening class had just been cancelled), ten weeks after starting writing and with over one hundred people signed up, the end is near. But we don't face the final curtain. Oh no. Although we're all doing it our way, we're going to keep on doing it, and do it some more.

An Age-Old Problem

I remember hearing Ian Rankin talking about writing on the occasion of his fiftieth birthday. He said that one of the great things about being a writer was the fact that age meant nothing, unlike in many other forms of entertainment. In fact, there's a case for saying that the older you get, the better you write. There's certainly no rush, especially if you're writing in the longer forms like fiction or memoir. Writing is a marathon, not a sprint. But just as you wouldn't attempt a marathon without training, you can't expect to suddenly sit down and complete a novel without at least a little limbering up first.

So, where now?

There are any number of places to go and things to do. Some cost money; some don't; have a look at all of them and decide which is the right step for you.

Study

The Open University runs a variety of Creative Writing courses, from introductory short units like 'Start Writing Fiction' [Start writing fiction (A174)] to full-blown degree-level courses like A215 Creative Writing (http://www.open.ac.uk/Arts/a215/index.html) and A363 Advanced Creative Writing (http://www3.open.ac.uk/study/undergraduate/course/a363.htm). But if all that sounds a bit too much, have a look at the BBC's Writersroom which has forums, writing tips and general support, in addition to the detailed advice you'll need if you're submitting to the BBC: http://www.bbc.co.uk/writersroom/.

Evening Classes

Although it was the cancellation of one such that sparked this course, creative writing courses and groups exist up and down the country and are often among the most popular at the institutions running them. You can view a directory of them here: http://www.hotcourses.com/uk-courses/Creative-Writing-courses/hc2_browse.pg_loc_tree/16180339/0/p_type_id/1/p_bcat_id/1617/page.htm

Websites
How To Write A Novel is about, well, how to write a novel but also so much more. Find it here: http://oldenoughnovel.blogspot.com/

Another site doing what it says on the banner is *Help! I Need a Publisher*. The book of the blog 'Write to Be Published' by Nicola Morgan (who knows what she's on about, with books almost into three figures) is out soon. Until then, check the blog here: http://helpineedapublisher.blogspot.com/

If inspiration ever wanes, a site like this - http://writeidea.wordpress.com/ - might come in handy. Linda Frear doesn't quite manage a different writing prompt each day, but she comes close.

One of the most comprehensive sites, constantly up-dated (I'm talking up to a dozen times daily!) and linking to writing sites all over the world is The Creative Penn: http://www.thecreativepenn.com/. If Joanna Penn doesn't cover it herself, she'll know somebody who does and she'll have linked to them, interviewed them or otherwise distributed their pearls of wisdom somewhere on her well-indexed site.

Publication

Getting published is both harder and easier than ever. The major publishing houses only rarely take on new talent, and the odds against getting an unsolicited manuscript to print are astronomical. But it does happen. Don't be daunted, and – most important of all – believe in your own work. After all, if you don't it's going to be harder to persuade someone else to.

There are alternatives – down to the printing of a single copy at so-called 'Espresso' machines – to traditional publishing. Small presses still thrive in a niche market, and the internet means that tiny publishers can have the same shop-window as the big boys (and girls) these days, with very little extra effort.

Then, of course, there's the future: eBooks. There seems little doubt that electronic publishing is not only here to stay, but it's going to keep on growing. Of course, there'll still be books and bookshops, but you've only got to look at the collapse of Borders earlier this year to realise that the old-fashioned way of doing things is becoming unsustainable. With smartphones, the iPad and a host of dedicated e-book readers, downloading a book is becoming as common as downloaded an album track. And look what iTunes has done for CD sales!

I think it's an exciting time to be an author. If you're prepared to look at alternative routes to publication, to embrace new technology and give up that dream of retiring on the royalties of your magnum opus, there's never been a better time to get your work into the hands of readers. And there's nothing like getting an email, out-of-the-blue, from someone, somewhere far away, who has read and enjoyed what you've written.

Isn't that what we're all in it for? Connecting with readers, communicating, sharing thoughts, ideas, and philosophies? As I started by saying ten weeks ago, we've all got something to say. Saying it in the most effective and entertaining way takes practice: and the practice – the writing, day-to-day, the revising, the editing, the polishing - is what most writers enjoy doing most. After all, if they didn't, they wouldn't be writers. Would they?

Summary

I hope you've enjoyed this short introduction to the world of creative writing. I've tried to cover as many topics as possible, and appeal to the broadest spectrum of would-be writers. Inevitably, I won't have said enough about somebody's favourite genre, or too much about something people aren't really interested in. But that's teaching!

Whatever your opinion, I hope you'll all keep writing!

Acknowledgements

The publishers would like to thank each of the authors for their contributions to this anthology, proceeds of which are being donated to the 2010 BBC Children in Need Charity Appeal.

Thanks also to Trish Burgess and Helen Hunt for their advice and support and to Dara Squires for setting up the online peer-support networks for the creative writing e-course.